No
Monsters
Allowed

Edited by
Alex Davis

Published by
Dog Horn Publishing
45 Monk Ings, Birstall, Batley WF17 9HU
United Kingdom
doghornpublishing.com

Edited by
Alex Davis

ISBN 978-1-907133-82-4

Cover art by
Justin Coons

Typesetting by
Jonathan Penton

UK Distribution: Central Books
99 Wallis Road, London, E9 5LN, United Kingdom
orders@centralbooks.com
Phone:+44 (0) 845 458 9911
Fax: +44 (0) 845 458 9912

Overseas Distribution: Printondemand-worldwide.com
9 Culley Court
Orton Southgate
Peterborough
PE2 6XD
Telephone: 01733 237867
Facsimile: 01733 234309
Email: info@printondemand-worldwide.com

No Monsters Allowed

INTRODUCTION

from Alex Davis

I have to start by saying that this is an anthology I have wanted to do for a long time. The title *No Monsters Allowed* has been rattling around in my head for many years, and the concept came around for a very simple reason – I can't remember the last time a monster really *scared* me in any form of fiction.

As a young horror reader I worked my way through many of the books that deliver classic monsters – James Herbert's *The Rats*, Stephen King's *IT* and of course the many Cthulhu tales of HP Lovecraft. I also saw more than my share of horror B-movies presenting all manner of weird and wonderful monsters.

However, over the course of time, I've very much found my taste changing towards what I've grown to dub 'human horror'. What another person can do to you can be just as terrifying – if not more so – than what any werewolf, vampire or zombie can inflict. For me, that comes from the feeling that you don't necessarily expect such a thing from your fellow human. The classic monsters, by their very definition, are evil. There's no shock when a zombie tries to eat your brains, a vampire tries to drink your blood, or a werewolf goes to bite and transform you. That's expected. A human being – well, human beings are surely *good*, on the whole? Aren't they?

Perhaps so. But you can't apply such a sweeping statement to all of humanity, and even less so when humanity finds itself placed in extreme situations. It's a common thread in what disparagingly gets called 'torture porn', a genre that for me has ironically brought some of the most affecting films of the last ten years. Movies like the Saw series, *Vile* and *The Tortured* have played with this concept in a manner that is both intelligent and harrowing. The fear doesn't come from the extreme nature of the violence itself, but the thought that it has been willingly inflicted by another person somewhere. There is also a lot to be said for the psychological aspect of horror – something foreign horror cinema does very ably, as evidenced by pieces such as *The Squad*, *Ringu* and *Hierro*.

What delighted me in particular with *No Monsters Allowed* is the range of submissions that I received. The term 'human horror' would of course seem to lend itself naturally to serial killers or revenge stories, but for me there is much more to it than that, something this anthology ably demonstrates. 'Bred in the Bone' and 'An Honest Woman's Child' tell of the horror of family relations that are broken beyond recognition. 'Puppyberries' and 'Special Girl' tell of the horrors that may lurk within childhood. 'Five an Hour' and 'The Algorithm' explore the horrors that lie within the human brain itself, under the right – or the wrong – circumstances. There are stories here that explore the horrors that can exist within the workplace, within politics, within friendships. Each of these stories takes a very different approach to its horror, but keeps the human element at the very heart.

So if the invasion of monsters has left you weary and jaded, there might just be something here to perk you up a bit.

And remember to just be that *bit* careful of the people around you...

Alex Davis
Wolverhampton, October 2013

TABLE OF CONTENTS

THE SMALL ONES HURT THE MOST
by Gary McMahon

I was eleven years old the first time I ever had my heart broken by a girl. Her name was Lucy Token – an unusual surname, but she was an unusual, and memorable, girl.

We went out for three weeks during the summer holidays. Back then, "going out" meant walking around together, holding hands, chalking our names on the footpaths and the sides of buildings, and telling anyone who would listen that we were madly and deeply in love.

After that short but blissful period of unutterable romance, she ditched me for a boy named Derek.

I was inconsolable for about a week, and then I started going out with my friends again. They'd thought of a new game that summer: it was called Play Dead.

In a couple of days I'd forgotten all about Lucy Token and how much she'd hurt me, and even when I saw her and Derek walking around the streets holding hands, the memory of her touch was as distant and impersonal as something I'd once seen in a film. At the time, I thought all the heartbreaks in my life would be this fleeting.

Play Dead was probably similar to the games played by every kid of that age, each version with his own variations on the theme. Our rules were simple, and they involved the Tucker Garages.

The Tucker Garages were a set of old asbestos garages located on a patch of waste ground a few hundred yards away from our house. They had not been used for storage in years, and had holes punched in the walls from two generations of kids throwing stones and kicking footballs.

The game involved one of us boys climbing up onto the roof of one of the garages and the rest standing below, in a line. One of the watchers would then assume a shooting stance, using a stick or a twig to simulate a gun. The type of firearm was dependent upon the size and shape of the stick, and whoever was up on the roof would have to fake their death scene with this in mind.

The shooter would pretend to shoot; the rooftop victim would then perform the most spectacular death scene possible. Things got really interesting when we started picking blackberries from the nearby bushes and using them as fake blood, which we'd spit from our mouths as we pirouetted one by one from the pitched roofs of the garages.

Lucy Token saw me performing there once. She and Derek were standing on the opposite side of the road, hand in hand. They stared at me as I took a swan dive, my mouth foaming with spittle and berry juice. When I stood up and brushed myself down, they were still there. Lucy smiled. She released her grip on Derek's hand. I turned away, feeling as if I'd claimed some sort of victory.

I thought about all of this as I stood in the shade of an old oak tree looking at the patch of ground where the Tucker Garages had once stood. I assumed the buildings had been condemned and torn down years ago, and there was a strange dull ache in my chest that told me I missed them, just like I missed so much else from my childhood.

"Happy?" said Lucy, who'd ditched Derek a long time ago; had become my girlfriend, and then my wife.

"Maudlin," I said, turning to her and smiling, just to let her know that I was okay, to show her that I was joking.

"Weird, isn't it, seeing the old neighbourhood like this?"

I nodded and turned back to the waste ground, seeing for a moment the fuzzy ghosts of a row of broken-down garage buildings. "Very. Whose great idea was it to come back here again?"

She squeezed my hand. Whenever she did that, I felt an echo of that sense of victory from years before, when she'd quietly and resolutely relinquished Derek's hand.

We continued along the street, past more boarded-up houses than I liked to see, and towards my mother's place. It was a week since the funeral and I'd been putting this off. If it were not for Lucy, I might have driven back to London and left the place to rot.

"It'll be fine," she said, as if reading my thoughts. "We go in, we sort out her stuff, and then we leave. One night max, and then it's home again, home again, jiggity-jig."

We did not stop at the gate; I reached out and pushed it open so that we could walk through without having to pause. I already had the keys in my hand as we approached the front door, and thankfully the door opened smoothly and easily when I unlocked it.

The hallway smelled of my mother: a combination of sour milk, fresh fish and air freshener. I felt my eyes prickling as we walked along the hallway, but I knew that if I raised my hand to my face my cheeks would be dry. I'd shed my tears for that woman long ago. I had no intention of crying for her ever again.

My mother was a neat and tidy woman. She'd organised her own funeral way before the bowel cancer took her, and her house reflected that same pathological desire to control every aspect of her existence. Everything was clean, there was little clutter, and all the paperwork was filed away using a system that even a child could understand.

As the sun went down outside, Lucy and I took the insurance documents, the house deeds, and any other form, missive or manuscript we thought we might need to conclude her affairs, and then we sat on the immaculate sofa in the depressingly Spartan lounge and realised that because we'd shared two bottles of Merlot as we worked, there was no way either one of us could drive the car.

"I can't sleep in her bed," I said, staring at the alcove where she'd point-blank refused to have a television. "It would feel… horrible."

"Don't worry," said Lucy. "I already thought of that. There's a sleeping bag and two pillows in the boot of the car."

I turned towards her, kissed her warm cheek, and then headed outside to get the gear.

We ordered takeaway from a local place – pizza, and it was a good one. Then we settled down to listen to the radio, which had been my mother's only source of entertainment other than the copious travel books she'd liked to read.

"She's gone now," said Lucy, curling into my side. "Don't be so tense. We buried her. She isn't coming back." She slipped her hand under my shirt and rubbed my belly, where the worst of the scars were still visible, and then she leaned over and kissed my neck.

"I know." I closed my eyes and tried not to think about all the bad things my crazy mother had done to me when I was a child. "But I feel like she's just hiding in here, waiting until I go to sleep."

"Don't be silly." She ran her hand along my thigh. "She's gone…long gone."

We undressed slowly and made love on the lounge floor. It wasn't great, but it was what we both needed to put my mother's ghost to rest. As I lay there afterwards, watching Lucy sleep, I remembered all the pain, the cuts and bruises, the burns and falls down the stairs. My mother had tortured me for years, but back then I'd had nobody to talk to about what was going on. My father had left us just a few weeks after I was born, the teachers at my school were cold and uncaring, and those child emergency telephone services did not exist. I was all alone, with her, and she used to hurt me.

That was the simple truth of the matter. The bitch used to hurt me.

I remembered again the games of Play Dead, when my friends and I would throw ourselves from those garage roofs, and I thought that maybe, just maybe the reason I always won was because I'd faked my own death a thousand times before. That was the only thing that made her stop: if I lay there, motionless, trying not to breathe, and she thought that she might have killed me. Only then would she stop whatever it was she was doing at the time; only then would she calm down and walk away, light a cigarette, pour herself a drink, retreat back inside herself that I could sneak up to my room to cry.

After the fact, it always seemed like she had no memory of what she'd done. She would ask me how school was, or if I wanted something to eat. She would send me to bed with hugs and kisses, and I'd lie awake for hours in case she decided to come upstairs for Round Two.

These thoughts running around in my head, I drifted off into a light doze. I think it was a sound that woke me. I can't be sure, even now, but I'm a heavy sleeper and don't usually wake up unless it's for something major.

"Lucy?"

She did not move. Her face was hidden by the top edge of the sleeping bag and both her arms were raised up over her head.

I decided not to disturb her, and slipped away from her side. I'd been sleeping on the floor, uncovered, so it was easy to move without having to touch her.

I went to the window and opened the curtains an inch or two. There was no one outside; the street was empty; the streetlights held the scene rigid in their cold electric glare.

Turning to face the room, I scanned the area. My mother had never owned a pet, so that couldn't be it. I remembered locking all the doors and checking the windows after coming in from the car that last time. Yet still, something had woken me.

I went out into the hallway and looked up the dark stairwell. Only shadows stirred. I reached out and switched on the light, and as I did so I thought I saw something make a twitchy retreat along the first floor landing.

Then I heard something. It was outside, on the street. Sounded like a heavy object slamming against the side of a car – maybe even my car. Forgetting what I thought I'd just seen, I turned and moved quickly towards the door, dragging it open and stepping outside into the warm night air.

There was nothing. No people, no traffic. It was just a quiet suburban street in the early hours of the morning. The pale moonlight reflected like frost on the windows of the houses as I moved slowly along the street, reluctant to investigate yet too afraid to go back without knowing what had made the noise.

I pictured a couple of bored teenagers out on a late-night prowl, kicking cars and running through gardens. We had done similar things when we were young. It was all just part of being a kid, playing silly games and making mischief.

The waste ground where the Tucker Garages no longer stood looked barren, as if some kind of catastrophe had occurred there. It was like a bomb site years after the explosion: the air still thrummed from the detonation, the earth vibrated softly if you got close enough to feel it. The lights from the airport flashed in the distance; I watched as a plane took off and diminished to nothing, not even a bright spot, in the sky.

I stepped over the low brick wall and stood staring at the place where the low asbestos garages had once been. Part of me expected to see them shimmering back into existence, with the ghost of my childhood self standing atop the roof like a king. That did not happen, of course. Things like that never happen in real life, only in stories.

I turned away and headed back towards the street and the deserted footpath. I felt eyes upon me, watching intently, but when I turned back the area was as still and silent as death. I made my way back to my mother's house, and only when I got there did the urge to leave come upon me with any great force. It would be so easy to pack up the stuff, wake Lucy and bundle her into the car, and then drive the two-hundred miles back to London. We'd be home before sunrise. We could crawl into bed and enjoy a lazy day, having unrushed sex and eating junk food from a duvet-picnic.

I went inside and shut the door behind me. Glancing up the stairs, I saw that nothing was moving. The light was off; I'd left it on when I had gone outside, but now the ground floor was in darkness

"Lucy?"

But I knew it wasn't her. It couldn't have been. If she was awake, she would have been waiting for me on the doorstep, wondering what the hell I thought I was doing out there in the dark.

Nervously, I went through into the lounge. The sleeping bag was an uneven bundle on the floor, and I knew without having to approach it that Lucy wasn't there. I went over anyway, just to be sure. To check that I wasn't being stupid.

She wasn't there. The bag was empty.

Lucy had a history of walking in her sleep, and because this was a strange house to her, it scared me that she might be roaming around in the dark. She might even hurt herself. Anything could happen.

"Where are you, honey?" My voice sounded high-pitched, childlike. I was regressing to a state I thought I'd left behind, a life I had escaped. But you can never get away; some things keep hold of you, not letting you go, never letting you leave. We die many times in our lives, practicing for the real thing, but it's always the small ones that hurt the most. The little deaths, those that happen over and over again, like a scream echoing inside an empty room.

I ran out into the hallway and turned to face the stairs. She was standing up there, on the landing. Her toes were hanging over the edge of the top step, and she was swaying gently from side to side.

"It's me, Lucy. Don't worry…it's okay, honey. Don't be afraid." I could not tell if she was asleep or awake. It was too dark, and I was

14

slightly too far away, to see if her eyes were open or closed.

I started to climb the stairs. There was nothing else that I could do. I had been called here, and I had come. My mistress had ordered me to heel, and like a beaten dog I'd obeyed her command without question.

Lucy started swaying even more violently, and in the darkness behind her I might have fooled myself that there was a figure, reaching out to push her. I blinked away the image, and then I focused on getting there, just reaching the top of the stairs so that I could save her. Nobody had ever been there for me, but I was here for her: I could do it; I could stop this.

"Wake up, honey. Come on, now, open your eyes." I'd heard it was dangerous to wake a somnambulist, but I was prepared to take the risk.

As I got closer, I saw her eyelids begin to flicker. Her mouth twitched, the lower lip drooping, spittle beading on her chin. She raised her hands to waist level, as if she were trying to regain her balance, but the darkness at her back surged forward, causing her to stagger.

I stopped.

Lucy's right foot slipped off the edge of the stair.

"Play dead," I whispered, not even understanding what I was saying or where the words had come from. "Play dead for me, honey…" I pictured a boy falling from a rooftop in glorious slow-motion, his mouth red with berry juice, and then I thought of that same boy lying prone on the kitchen floor, his right eye already swelling and his belly slashed to pink and red ribbons by a steak knife. A small, defeated boy pretending to be dead until the bad lady lost interest and went away.

As Lucy fell I tried to catch her, but by then it was already too late. If she'd simply played dead, as I'd asked, she might still be alive now. That's what I tell myself when it gets too dark to see and when the walls of the bedroom we once shared begin to move in towards me, threatening to crush the life out of me.

She fell past me, slamming against the wall on her way to the bottom. I heard the hollow sound of impact as her head hit the bricks, and then she was gone, gone, gone…

I lifted my head and stared at the peculiar density of darkness at the top of the stairs. It seemed to throb gently, and then, a second later, it was just the darkness again. My mother was not there, watching me from the upper floor, and the fear I'd experienced was all of my own making, filling me like bile, spilling out to pollute the air when I got too full.

I didn't need any more ghosts. I already had the phantoms of my past to torment me.

I stumbled down the stairs and kneeled down beside Lucy, holding her broken hands and calling her name. But it was no use; none of it helped. She was gone; I had lost her. Maybe she was never really mine to begin with, and I'd just borrowed her for a while, until the abuses of my past finally caught up with me and took her away.

Lucy had lost the game; her performance had not rung true. She would never climb up there again, and I'd never get to see if she could fall properly, the way I had fallen so many times when I was a child.

I lowered my head and started to cry.

Then I did the only thing I could think of in that frantic, near-insane moment: I lay down on the floor, curling my body around hers, and I played dead for one last time until daybreak.

Gary McMahon is the acclaimed author of seven novels. His short fiction has been reprinted in several Year's Best volumes. He lives with his family in Yorkshire, where he trains in Shotokan karate and likes running in the rain. Website: www.garymcmahon.com

THE SILENCE AFTER WINTER
by Adam Craig

It looked alien against the dun browns of raw earth, the ashen greys of dying vegetation. A sour wind kicked up a plume of dust and she clutched a gloved hand over her face, nose pinched shut. The silence was broken only by the girl's stifled coughing.

"D-do you think …"

"Shush." She kept her voice low, the word muffled further by layers of bandannas and the face mask digging into her cheeks. Her eyes wandered again over the farmhouse, searching for resolve. "Wait here. I won't be long."

The tilt of the girl's head suggested she wanted to argue. Then, shoulders jerking as a fresh cough was swallowed, the girl simply hunkered lower behind the small stand of bushes they were crouching beside. The twisted branches, mottled with spreading mould, offered a meagre hiding place.

She looked at the girl a moment, and then walked cautiously beyond the breast of the hill. Only stifled coughing followed her.

A wisp of smoke drifted exhaustedly from the farmhouse. Windows black like eye patches, roof broken by a fire that must have burned out only a few hours ago. From the hillside, there was no sign of the fighting she had heard the previous night. Nothing to show the farmhouse had not stood lifeless for months. Nothing but guttering smoke.

She paused, absently rubbing dust from her goggles. There seemed little point in going closer. Nothing useful could have survived.

They had heard the gunshots while sheltering in the car. Vents and doors crudely taped shut; the sound was muted to a series of dull claps. Huddled in the back seat, they had stared into the darkness as a second ragged burst drifted on the wind.

"Are they close?" The girl's eyes were just visible in the gloom, the balance of her face hidden behind a dirty face mask.

No answer, only an unspoken hope the shooting was a long way off.

"Are we safe?" The girl's voice caught.

She looked into the darkness. Belatedly, she thought to put an arm around the girl. "Of course we're safe."

She had no idea if this was true.

Eventually, the girl slept. The gunshots went on, growing sporadic before petering out entirely. Unbroken quiet settled around the abandoned car, although she continued staring through the windows into the darkness.

She awoke with a start. A flickering touch of orange brought false dawn to the sky. Flames. For a moment, while sleep still lingered, she thought they were back at the burning city, that it was still winter.

Mist softened the desolation, drawing the land into itself so that mouldering vegetation and pearly air almost merged. She helped the girl from the car, hesitating before gently pushing the door closed, pausing in case even that much sound was too much, in case there was anyone to hear. They walked up the road. Beneath swathes of scarves and yellow-eyed goggles, the girl looked more frail this morning. Each cough was brittle in the stillness.

They saw the body ahead of them again.

"I thought ..." The girl pointed back beyond the car towards the sundered remains of a fallen tree.

"No." She pointed in the opposite direction to one the girl was now facing. "This way." Her voice was confident, belying the truth. This might have been the direction they had been travelling yesterday; they might be going back on themselves. It hardly mattered. All she hoped was to go anywhere but towards last night's gunfire.

They settled into a steady plod. Every direction looked much the same. Except for the body. Face pressed into the verge, one arm blindly flung out. Seemingly pointing the way. Fungus dressed the remains, hiding any lingering trace of identity or hint of exposed bone under a soft shroud. The miasma hanging around the road had nothing to do with the body, but she placed a gloved hand over her lower face just the same.

Later, after the mist had burned away to leave a featureless spring sky, she trudged up the hill and saw the farmhouse below. All directions seemed to lead to the same end now.

She had no idea how long they had been wandering when they found the burning city.

Working desperately against the fading winter's day, they had struggled to get into the bungalow. Heavily boarded-up against its owners' unrealised hopes of return, the building appeared not to have been touched since their departure. She beat the hammer against the planks nailed across the grimy front door. The impacts echoed, almost dying before the next blow. Breath came in gasps, pale against the dejected afternoon, leaving the inside of her face mask clammy. After a time, the girl wordlessly took the hammer and bashed clumsily at wood, doorframe, handle. Even with exertion, the afternoon was cold. It felt like snow and the girl was shivering by the time the door yielded.

A single bottle of water lay in the fridge. It was the first luck they had had since the girl developed her cough, become sickly. Otherwise, the cupboards were stripped but for a few tins of fruit. Little else seemed to have been taken, provisions more important than possessions. It was sheer miracle that the house had not been looted before now. The girl's smile of delight showed over the top of the clinging scarves.

Despite being well shuttered, a fine layer of dust covered every surface. Slowly, she drew a gloved finger through the film. Wondering: how much was simply dust, how much of fungal spores?

Cross-legged in front of the silent fridge, they put on fresh bikini masks. Only a few remained in her backpack and she tried not to worry where they might find more. Then, water bottle between them, they shared a tin of fruit. Breath held to lift the mask, slurp at the water, nibble fruit so brightly coloured it seemed to belong to some other world.

She smiled around her own mask at the girl.

Darkness came quickly inside the shuttered bungalow. She paused, about to risk switching on the wind-up torch, when a flicker of light caught her eye. A gap in the boards, high up, beyond standing eye-height. Stunned seconds passed before she helped the girl up on to the cupboard-top and they pressed their faces to the cold glass.

It looked like street-lighting.

How many nights had gone unbroken, or eased only by the moon? She had never realised just how dark the night was. Long, winter's nights. And now this. Distant, but strong enough to stain the sky a sodium orange.

Neither noticed the shiftless flickering painting and re-painting the fast-closing night. Hope made them blind to that.

Next morning, they found themselves running. Across a field grown marshy with rot to stumble and crash headlong through a stand of dying trees. Where blackthorn and briar might have made the way impassable, there was now only blight. The reek of decay went unnoticed, attention centred on glimmers of light visible between the softening boles, escaping from beneath a press of heavy cloud.

The smoke looked yellow through the goggles. Flames limned the horizon, giving the land an autumnal sheen which it had been incapable of mustering itself this year. The smell of soot was bitter despite filtering layers of cloth.

She had looked around. Aside from the flames, the landscape was anonymous. Mould coated what had not been stripped bare by the winds. Everywhere now looked the same. She had no idea what this burning town was called.

She had no idea where they were any more.

The butterflies returned with the spring.

The insects had disappeared over the long, bleak winter. Now the sunshine was growing warmer, they began to flit across the barren countryside again.

Sweating a little beneath her wrappings, she paused to watch two of the butterflies wander by. They should have been an indicator of renewal, rebirth or something, those butterflies. Brilliant, iridescent wings fluttering in spring sunshine.

The girl instinctively shied away from them. Their wings seemed too bright amid the drab landscape, flickers of unnatural colour where brown and grey were the norm. She put an arm around the girl, feeling nervous around the insects herself despite her muffled words of reassurance.

Turning, she gently led the girl away. Threading between the potholes, ice-shattered tarmac crunched underfoot as they trudged uphill again. Any direction was better than being near the butterflies.

She looked back, once. The butterflies wafted down to settle on a broad rash of fungus that smothered what might once have been a roadside flower display. Splayed wings gaudy against the faintly hairy rot as they began to feed. The sallow vegetation yet to succumb to the fungus held no interest for them.

Days slowly lengthened.

In some ways, nothing changed. They still wandered. As much as during the winter. Only the silence was worse. Spring should not be a time of silence.

Lampposts stood forlornly on either side of the road. The verge had disappeared, reduced to black stains like bruises against earth become naked, bright sunshine making no difference. A hedge straggled away from the road, sagging under its own festering weight as it roved across an otherwise barren field. A redundant fence-line rose on the opposite side to stop a small cluster of houses from coming any closer. Beyond them, more houses coalesced into a town.

"Is this …" The girl struggled for a name.

"I think we're in …" Each house stood firm beneath smears of dirt, a single winter of neglect not enough to bring much damage. A few broken windows, some missing roof tiles. Nothing much. No weeds marred the block paving forming the curtilage of each dwelling, household perfection achieved by error. "No, I think this is …" She shrugged. Names no longer mattered.

With unspoken agreement, they skirted the edges of the town. It looked deserted, but there was no sense taking chances. Only later did they backtrack to any of the untenanted buildings. Nervous of being trapped, expecting horrors. Finding nothing but stillness, a silence they hardly disturbed. Confidence rising, they

21

wandered the length of the road: trying shop doors, peeking through letter boxes, climbing stairs far enough to peer through banister rails at what lay beyond.

Spores mottled almost every surface, taking hold in some places to become a thick mat of grizzled fibres. Pickings were rich enough, even so, enough to keep them going.

She willingly let the pressure of the silence push them out of the town, relieved to be moving again. It was better to be moving, even if there was no idea of destination at the end.

The girl's cough was worse that night. Each heave racked the girl's increasingly thin frame. She sat to one side, sometimes placing an arm around the girl's heaving shoulders. She told herself she could feel something. But there was only emptiness inside, as if the empty countryside had somehow seeped in and replaced all that had once been there.

He stood in the middle of the road. A single wave, then a long wait as they decided whether to approach or not.

Swathed in scarves, his face was a mystery. The girl hid behind her, unwilling to look at the stranger. He held out empty hands, gloves seeming odd in the warm sunshine.

"I've not seen anyone in ages."

She said nothing in reply, cold now despite protective layers. The girl clutched at her hand.

"Could I walk with you?" His voice sounded strange, too loud. Nervous too, she thought. "Just for a bit?"

A butterfly wandered past. Scattered clouds hung, grey-white against blue. Sunlight warm, growing warmer as they stood in the stillness. The silence.

The urge to run was painful. She tried to meet his gaze. Dusty goggles obscured his eyes, her own turning the afternoon amber. Contact was impossible, if only because her distrust placed so much distance between them.

In the end she simply started walking. The girl scuttled ahead, breath hoarse with eagerness to be away from the stranger. They climbed to the top of a steep embankment. A motorway cut an artificial valley beneath them. The wind hummed along its length, spinning dust devils only to let them settle forgotten on the tarmac.

Wind-blown earth and spores lay in drifts across the road surface. Slowly, the motorway was vanishing.

Turning, they let the ridgeline lead them in parallel to the abandoned road. When the stranger caught up and began walking beside them, she said nothing.

They wandered through a small industrial estate. Warehouses kept mute company with small garages and engineering sheds become desolate. The road sounded gritty beneath their feet. Bending sharply. Revealing a curtain-wall of prime movers and overturned trailers surrounding one warehouse. Halting, she waved the man back. The girl needed no warning; she was already looking for a way off the main road, a back-route that would get them away from whoever hid behind that barrier.

The man ignored her. He stood, only half-concealed by a sign advertising amazing reductions on tyres that would never be repeated, and looking at the fortified warehouse.

"I think ..." he began, and then crossed the road to climb over the metal ramparts.

She did not wait. Turning, she took the girl's hand and helped search for escape.

He found them trying to wrench a gap in a sagging chain-link fence.

"It's empty." Beckoning, he led them back to the fortified warehouse. Doors gaped, windows casting back fractured reflections of the spring sunshine. Inside, the signs of fighting seemed out of place in the stillness of the cavernous space. Burst water bottles lay amid a sparse chaff of dropped cans and ruptured sacks of breakfast cereal.

Strangely, despite her timidity, it was the girl who found it. Certain the fortified warehouse was abandoned, she relaxed, only to realise the girl had wandered off. The sound of muffled coughing floated through the derelict, then vanished. She listened for a while longer and, when no shouts or screams broke the silence, allowed herself to relax once again.

She watched the man pick through the little left by whoever had invaded this place. Not much was of use. Abstractly, she felt her stomach tighten. Usually hunger was so constant it was unnoticeable.

Then, the girl returned. Panting, excited coughing making it impossible to do anything other than point.

It might once have been a storeroom. Tucked behind the warehouse but not actually part of. A high roller door, allowing vehicles access to the interior, stood beside a reinforced door flanked by two windows. The roller door refused to move or even rattle to the touch; the pedestrian doorway was equally stubborn. Shrouds of plastic blinded the windows, but not so well that a narrow chink did not offer a glimpse of what lay inside.

"Oh my god." The man stood back, the tilt of his head betraying shock. Eagerness, too.

She stepped around him, gloved hands blocking out daylight, peered through the window. The door led into some sort of small room. Shrouds of plastic blocked most of the view of the space beyond. Most seemed to be in shadows, except for a shaft of sunlight from an unseen skylight picking out part of the side of a box: –AKED BEA–

Despite the barrenness that lay inside her, the sight brought a thrill.

Breaking in was a trial. Taking turns, they beat against the pedestrian door with a length of metal fence post and a chunk of concrete prised from the service road running down the side of the main warehouse. Sweat poured under protective layers, the air filtering through the face mask too little to manage with. And the noise of the hammering was terrible. As she beat against the locks, she felt hackles rise, her scalp tight with the fear of discovery. Agitated and too weak to help further, the girl stood a nervous watch at the end of the service road.

The only thing that came by was a butterfly.

Still, the relief when the door finally burst inwards was only matched by the shock at finding the place piled high with supplies. Tinned food, water, medical supplies, even some camping equipment.

Riches greater than mere money.

Dust brushed and washed away as best as possible, they sealed themselves inside the storeroom. The building was tall but relatively narrow and short: a main space, served by the roller doors, where the supplies were piled on the floor and lines of narrow metal shelves along the walls; an alcove at the back and the small anteroom-cum-entrance hall immediately behind the pedestrian doorway. The roller door was welded shut, its edges sealed with cumbersome lines of mastic, the whole covered over with a long plastic sheet. A second sheet hung loosely across the alcove at the rear, a third blocking the entrance to the anteroom and the only working exterior door. The storeroom had been well prepared.

Shaking away the last dust from her external clothing, she stepped inside and they closed the door. Bits of metal and wood covered the splintered jamb, held in place with sealant and lots of tape. The lock no longer worked but the spindle still moved when the handle turned, latching against their repairs. Then fresh sealant from the stocks on the shelves, gobs running thick down the crack between door and jam. The place as tight as it was possible to be.

Quickly, she stripped away a few intermediate layers, placing them in a black plastic sack and trying not to think of what she might have ingested before now. The girl looked strange without scarves and goggles. Frailer, wan in the glow from the skylights. They had all eaten and drank more in the day since they had broken in than they had had in … some time. The girl seemed better for it, although her cough had racked long into the night just past.

The man found paper, a pen, a wind-up torch. Methodically, he inventoried their gold mine of supplies. Skin hung loosely around his pale face, suggesting he might have been fuller and fatter before. She watched him abstractly: small, tight handwriting; opening each box, moving from shelf to shelf to each pile heaped in the corners; the look of concentration lending some depth to an otherwise unmemorable face.

He was still working when she fell asleep.

"Are you her mother? You never said." He looked up from the sheets of neat writing. Overhead, the skylights were bright rectangles amid the shadows. The girl was sleeping in the small alcove at the rear of the storeroom. For all she could tell, he had worked through the night.

"I knew her father. Met her mother once. Twice. I don't

remember."

"You care about her, though." There was something in his voice, a need she could not identify.

She opened her mouth but could think of nothing to say. Instead, she went into the anteroom beside the pedestrian door and folded aside the plastic sheeting covering one of the windows. The storeroom lay just inside the perimeter of the industrial estate. A security fence, backed by a row of fragile silver birches, separated the estate from a gently sloping field which was confined behind a stand of trees marking the start of a large, dilapidated estate of houses.

Mould sprawled out from the line of birches, coating the field and creeping through the second line of trees. A spongy desert that saw no need to conform to old boundaries. The sun shone on the rot, glinting through the blackened branches from the vacant, dusty windows of the houses. Silence hung heavily.

In films or TV, when a woman, a child and a man found each other like this, they went off into the countryside. Started afresh.

She watched the sunlight shimmer from the colourful wings of the butterflies as they fed on the mould and felt nothing.

That afternoon, clouds filled the sky and it began to rain. The noise was shocking after the silence, drumming against the metal roof until the walls throbbed.

She sat in the alcove, holding the girl, who was scared by the sound. The arms clasping her waist were little more than bone. Darkness filled the storeroom, broken only by the flash of a torch as the man carried on listing every item he could find in the building. Now and then, he would pause and leaf through the crumpled sheets of writing as if worried he had overlooked something.

The rain lost some of its strength and the girl's sobbing waned into sleep. After a time, she slipped out from under the girl and went again to peer through the windows. Grey sludge ran in the gutters, spatters of decay griming the lower walls of the warehouse on the opposite side of the service road.

She stared out for a long time before she realised that the rain itself was grey. Tainted as it fell from a sky heavy with invisible spores and blight.

After several revisions, he finally let her see the inventory. The obsession that had carried him around the densely-stocked storeroom three times set an odd cast to his face, weak sunlight dropping through the skylights to dip his eyes in shadow.

"There's plenty." He took back the sheets, reordered them, and paused as if torn, then handed them back to her.

She leafed through, entries underscored and written over repeatedly until it was hard to make out exactly what he had counted.

He gently touched the uppermost sheet, like someone petting a favourite cat. "For now. In fact, I reckon we could support a few more people. You know, survivors like us."

From somewhere behind them, the sound of the girl moving around was punctuated by racking coughs, each ending in an odd gurgle.

"Children like your daught— the girl and, and that. A community. There'd be hands then. To help. Move, I mean. Somewhere bigger. And scavenge. Get supplies, make a go of it." He stared uncomprehendingly at her blank expression. "I don't think this, this fungus stuff is, you know, *everywhere,* do you? I mean, the telly and the papers, they exaggerated, didn't they? Like, for sales and that. The rot can't be everywhere. Can it …"

She watched shadows move across his face. Revealing a little, hiding something else. She and the girl might have wandered miles and miles, but everywhere was the same. Before, before it all stopped and there was no more TV, no more of anything, the news had said the blight and the butterflies had already appeared in lots of countries. At first, new pesticides and GM crops had been blamed for both the insects and the mould, but these new places had apparently used neither. She thought about saying this, but the effort felt too much. Instead, she silently held out the inventory until he reluctantly took it back.

"Well," he said, fingering the sheets, "think about it."

Later, the weather turned fine again. Gradually, the storeroom began to feel almost warm enough to take off the last few layers of clothing and expose more than the bare minimum of skin to the air. She stood by the windows, gazing through the kink in the plastic sheets. The man's voice mumbled unintelligibly from some corner of the room, the girl's answers as impossible to divine. Instead of going to see what they were doing, she simply watched the butterflies mobbing one of the sagging birches just the other side of the security fence. A gaily coloured cloud of the insects settled on several withered branches, wings twitching in the sunshine.

Without warning, the whole tree fell in on itself in a cloud of startled butterflies. Plumes of mottled dust roiled towards the cloudless sky, seeming to hang motionless on the still air for hours afterwards.

Only the butterflies moved.

"I'm going out again." He folded and refolded the sheets of inventory as he spoke. "Tomorrow, I mean."

He tried to catch her eye, but she pretended to be busy crushing aspirin for the girl. She could see him fingering the storeroom inventory, carefully lining up the edges and smoothing out the creases over and over.

"To look for survivors," he added at last.

She looked at him then, although no reply suggested itself. Before she could search for one, the girl began coughing. The cough had worsened over the afternoon, becoming hacking with the onset of night and rapidly falling temperatures. The storeroom was cold now, dark but for the wind-up lanterns. She turned back to the medicine. No food; the girl could only keep down aspirin, her temperature climbing as the room grew chill.

"It's — I —" He stammered, tongue as unable to latch on to words as her own. Finally, he sighed. "Have to try. It's a, a duty."

The sound of the wind woke her. The girl's head cradled in her lap, forehead burning to the touch. Each rasping breath sent a soft vibration through her leg. She slid gently from under the girl's head, cushioning it on an inflatable pillow. On the opposite side of the alcove, the man lay on his back, mouth gaping, snores almost inaudible above the wind.

She looked up at the skylights, pale grey rectangles in the

darkness of the roof. It might be imagination, but she could hear spores pattering on the scuffed plastic, the wind trying to push them around the taped-up windows, under the door. She could almost see them glowing as they drifted on the still air inside the storeroom.

Except she knew the mould did not glow. Not even when it bloomed.

She listened to the wind and thought how safe this place felt after so long spent wandering. She did not want to consider going outside again, not even though she knew these supplies could not last forever. They had to run out eventually. There was no need for more people to come here to see that happen …

It was such a strange idea that she could not imagine it somehow: people from outside. Outside was silence and butterflies. It was grey and black. Putrid and empty. There couldn't be anyone else.

She had been thinking the exact same thing when they met the man.

The wind roused itself into a fresh gust. The girl stirred, murmurs turning bronchial, congested.

She knelt, laying a hand lightly on hot forehead. Caring, she realised, was an odd thing. It stole over you without notice. Just when you felt numb and insulated — from shock and pain, from the empty world outside — you realised what you stood to lose. What mattered. What hurt.

Another gust rumbled down the service road. She stroked the girl's hair until sleep deepened and the child relaxed. Darkness, wind, the sound of breathing between gusts. Shapes standing motionless in the darkness, each one listed on the man's crumpled inventory.

She sat, stroking the girl's hair and turning things over for a long time. Finally, she got up and walked towards the sleeping man.

Sunlight made brilliant squares of the skylights. She paused in the middle of winding on the last scarf to go back and check the girl again. Sleeping peacefully, each shallow breath flattened by the walls of the alcove. Perhaps that was the only reason they sounded wrong. Gently, she laid a hand on the girl's forehead. There was no need of a thermometer. Touch alone was enough to tell her how high the girl's temperature was.

Not allowing herself to think on any further, she taped the plastic curtain down across the mouth of the alcove. Pulling on gloves, she stood outside the anteroom leading to the pedestrian door. The man's body was visible through the falls of plastic covering the arch. Her eyes slid from it to the pedestrian door. Time passed while she breathed and searched for strength, courage. At last, she ducked under the plastic and began stripping away the tape and sealant around the edges of the pedestrian door.

Her hands shook, fingers hard to control. Going outside again was almost impossible. By comparison, what she had done last night — taking up a pillow, kneeling beside the man as he slept until she could stand the tension no longer — that had been easy. Even afterwards, dragging him into the anteroom and listening to the wind die back as the sun returned, had been easy. But going outside …

Once she passed out of the shadow of the warehouse on the opposite side of the service road, the day became very warm. Almost like summer. Panting, she rested for a few minutes. A butterfly wove along the edge of the gutter before settling on a heap of fungus occupying an otherwise bare strip of earth marked out by a series of concrete blocks. Sometime, some long ago time, it had probably been a flower-bed. She looked away, up into the sky. Nothing marred that, not even a single cloud. Azure, without a hint of any taint. Perhaps the rain and the wind had washed it clean. She put the thought aside as she picked up his arms and began dragging again.

The girl lived just long enough for the storeroom to lose the edge off its chill as the weather remained warm and sunny. Long enough for them both to roll up sleeves, shed the last few protective layers and leave skin bare to the atmosphere. It had been a strange few days. Certainly the oddest since they had started wandering.

Gently, so very gently, she wrapped the girl in the plastic curtain that had hung across the alcove's mouth. Kissed her forehead before binding the shroud with tape. Not one tear, though. It seemed too late for that.

The sheets of plastic across the windows beside the pedestrian door came down with surprisingly little effort. Sunlight filled the service road, streaming through now bare windows. Standing in its warmth, she watched the sun rise each morning until the corner of the warehouse opposite finally hid it from view.

This morning, she held her bare arms up to the light. The blotches did not look so bad like this, less grey, less malignant. A tickle had developed in her throat overnight, refusing to shift no matter how much she drank. Without any emotion, she supposed the cough would set in tomorrow, the day after perhaps. The thought of what was spreading inside her hardly bothered her. It seemed too late to shed tears over that, too.

Instead, she rested her fingers on the door handle and watched the butterflies dancing in the sunlight.

*This is **Adam Craig**'s first published story; the surprise has yet to wear off. If you're filled with an inexplicable but nonetheless compelling urge to communicate, he'd be tickled if you'd e-mail him at adamcraigsmail@ gmail.com.*

CANVASSING OPINION
by Stuart Hughes

On a soft pre-election evening in April 2010, a young woman turned the corner and walked briskly into Sculptures Close. She wore a dark grey suit with matching jacket and knee-length skirt, the narrow party tie worn smartly, the knot tight against the collar of her freshly pressed white shirt. Her hair was strawberry blonde and tied back in a long ponytail. Her skin tone was fair, her eyes a greyish-green, bright red lipstick neatly applied to her lips. She sported a brightly coloured rosette on her left breast.

Sculptures Close was a cul-de-sac with a mix of two, three and four-bedroom houses giving it a particularly pleasing look. The houses ran alternately – odd numbers on the right-hand side and even numbers on the left. Sculptures Close was important for the local campaign this general election. The majority of residents had placed their X in favour of an opposing candidate at the last election. Canvassing here would help to build up a picture of whether there would be a sufficient swing this time round to win the parliamentary seat for Mid-Derbyshire.

The young woman looked at the clipboard she carried in her left hand. Number 1 Sculptures Close. Mr and Mrs Brookes, married, both fifty-three. The party had no information on how they had voted last time. Finding out how they would vote on Thursday 6th May was crucial to the local campaign.

She knocked on the front door and almost immediately heard footsteps coming towards her. The front door opened to reveal a large woman wearing a white blouse and a long black skirt.

"Mrs Brookes?" she asked politely.

"That's right."

"Good evening, Mrs Brookes. I'm sorry to disturb you this evening but I'm canvassing opinion on the forthcoming general election. Would you mind telling me how you intend to vote?"

Mrs Brookes looked at the young woman with friendly green eyes, glanced at her rosette, and then looked at her again.

"As you're so pretty," she smiled, "I'll tell you. I voted for your party. My husband and I have already voted by post."

"And Mr Brookes?"

"He's still at work, but I know he voted the same as me."

"Thank you," the young woman said. "Thank you for your support." She began walking down the drive.

"Good luck."

The young woman stopped for a moment, gave a broad smile, and lifted her hand in a wave.

Mrs Brookes waved back, grinned, and closed the door.

When she got to the end of the drive, the young woman stopped, placed a tick by the names of Mr and Mrs Brookes, and checked the details for the next house. Number 3, Mr Savage, a gentleman in his mid-sixties, a widower who had lived on his own since his wife's death. He had been a staunch supporter last time round. If they were going to achieve the necessary swing, the party needed his staunch support again.

She turned into the drive of 3 Sculptures Close and hurried towards the house with a skip and a dance and that same broad smile on her lips.

The young woman pressed the doorbell with the forefinger of her right hand and listened to the muffled chimes. She waited. She didn't have to wait long.

The front door opened and the young woman smiled. Mr Savage wore a torn, green knitted sweater and brown slacks. His face was a map of wrinkles, his brown eyes were deep in pouches, and a cigarette jittered between his nicotine-stained fingers.

"Mr Savage?" the young woman asked politely.

"Yeah."

"Good evening, Mr Savage. I'm canvassing opinion for the forthcoming general election. Would you mind telling me how you intend to vote?"

Mr Savage coughed loudly, spraying germs.

The broad smile never quivered on the young woman's lips. She looked into the deep-set eyes of Mr Savage, saw the retired man's gaze shift in the direction of her rosette for a moment – or maybe her breasts – before resuming eye contact.

"Since you're wearing the right colour, my dear, I don't mind telling you at all. I'm going to be voting for your mob."

"Thank you. Any particular reason why?"

"You know why, my pretty friend, don't you?"

The young woman nodded.

"Country's in a right mess. Bloody shambles, ain't it? You know it and I know it. Get the buggers out and let's have somebody with some common sense running the country for a change."

"I agree with you wholeheartedly, Mr Savage." The young woman extended her right hand.

"Call me Ernie," Mr Savage said and shook the young woman's hand.

"Thank you for your support, Ernie."

"You're welcome." Mr Savage grinned, displaying two rows of stained and missing teeth. "I think you'll have your work cut out for you tonight though, my dear."

"Your neighbours?"

"My neighbours, yeah. Nice people, most of them, but blind as bats. Can't see beyond the end of their own noses. Can't see the bloody mess this country's in."

The young woman giggled like a schoolgirl at that.

"I'm only telling you what I think, my dear. Advice doesn't cost owt, does it?"

"It's about the only thing that doesn't with this government in power."

"You can say that again."

The young woman smiled her broad smile. "Don't you worry about your neighbours, Mr Savage. Some of them might surprise you."

"I doubt it. I know your mob offers the best hope for this country but they just can't see it."

"That's why I'm here, Ernie." The young woman's smile stretched even broader as she raised her hand in a wave.

Mr Savage closed the door and the young woman walked away. At the end of the drive she stopped and placed a tick against the name of Mr Savage. She checked the details for the next house. 5 Sculptures Close. Mr and Mrs Lewis. A married couple, him thirty-five, her thirty-two. Both voted for the government last time round. Knowing how they intended to vote this year would be important.

She turned into the drive and skipped and danced towards the Lewis house.

The young woman rapped on the door with the knuckles of her right hand. She waited. She waited a while longer. Rapped again.

"Coming! Coming!" A deep voice boomed out. "Hold your horses!"

The front door opened and the young woman smiled broadly. Mr Lewis wore black denim jeans and an unbuttoned grey shirt. He was barefoot.

"Mr Lewis?" the young woman asked politely.

"Yes." He checked her out, up and down, his eyes lingering on her breasts.

"Good evening, sir. Sorry to disturb you, but I'm canvassing opinion for the forthcoming general election. Would you mind telling me how you intend to vote?"

"Yes, I would mind."

"May I assume, then, that you won't be voting for us?" The young woman's smile fluttered briefly and she felt a moment's disharmony.

"That's correct."

"May I ask why?"

"None of your damned business."

The young woman reached inside her jacket pocket and pulled out a pin hammer.

Mr Lewis backed away, his mouth wide open in surprise, blood visibly draining away from his face. Mr Lewis tried to close the door but the young woman was too quick for him, blocking it with her body.

"Who is it honey?" a soft, female voiced called from upstairs.

The young woman swung the pin hammer and struck Mr Lewis on his temple. She swung the hammer and struck him again, swung and struck again, swung and struck...

Mr Lewis slumped to the floor and the young woman followed him down, straddling his chest, swinging and striking with the hammer, swinging and striking, swinging and striking...

She heard a scream.

The young woman looked up to see a blur of motion –

sweeping brunette hair, a flowery dressing gown flapping against naked legs – hurrying up the stairs.

"Mrs Lewis?"

The young woman stepped inside the house.

"I'm canvassing opinion for the forthcoming election," she said and hurried up the stairs.

Later that soft pre-election evening the young woman slipped the pin hammer back inside her jacket pocket, stepped over the body of Mr Lewis, and closed the front door after her. She skipped and danced down the drive.

The evening was getting darker now, but it was still beautiful. If there were bloodstains on her dark grey suit they wouldn't show much, not in the twilight of a soft late April evening.

At the end of the drive she stopped and crossed out the names of Mr and Mrs Lewis. She checked the details for the next house. Amanda Carsley. Miss Carsley. Aged twenty-four. Miss Carsley was renting the property from a Mr and Mrs Stow who were living and working abroad on a five year contract. Miss Amanda Carsley was a crucial voter; according to party information she was a dangerous floater.

Miss Carsley might need some persuading.

The young woman began to smile. She reached inside her jacket pocket and caressed the pin hammer.

She skipped and danced her way up the drive towards Miss Carsley's front door.

Stuart Hughes was born in Burton upon Trent in March 1965. He started writing seriously in 1988 and his first short story was published a year later. Since then he has had over 50 short story credits in various magazines and anthologies. For nine years Stuart edited the award winning magazine Peeping Tom, *which won the British Fantasy Award in 1991 and 1992. In 1997, eleven of his short stories were published in the collection* Ocean Eyes. *A collection of stories he collaborated on with D. F. Lewis titled* Busy Blood *(theEXAGGERATEDpress) was published in 2012. A second collection of his short stories will be published by theEXAGGERATEDpress in 2013. TheEXAGGERATEDpress will also publish a definitive collection of Stuart Hughes short stories in 2014.*

Some Girls Wander by Mistake

by Amelia Mangan

Music pounded off grimy white tiles, shook the cracked bathroom mirrors, slammed and swam and twisted through Jack Kelloway's skull as the last of the cocaine vanished up his right nostril. A shuddered breath escaped his lips; his head fell back; colored lights flashed and glittered in the dark. He could feel it, glistening granules tumbling through his bloodstream, lighting up his brain. He'd be up all night, and that was how he wanted it.

He remembered the first time he'd ever done coke. His big brother, Nick. Twenty-one at the time. Jack had been eleven. He traced the curves of his lips, remembering how Nick had taken him by the chin, fingertips grazing his right cheekbone, and kissed the drug into his mouth. He'd felt as if his head were about to leave his shoulders, as if his body were water.

Sometimes Jack thought he could still hear Nick, still see him – in the early hours of the dawn, in the hush and cold before birds began twittering outside the window and cars started whispering beyond the curtain, when the whole world was darkness and quiet breathing. But Nick was gone. Long gone. A couple of years after he'd first started paying special attention to Jack he'd jumped in front of a truck. Just went and did it. No note or anything. Jack could never figure out why. Maybe he'd let him down.

He didn't know how he could've done that, though. It wasn't as if what they'd done made him gay or anything. No, he wasn't gay. He knew that for sure.

He knew that because of the girls. The lovely, lovely little girls.

It was hard to remember their names now, though sometimes they'd come back to him at odd moments. He'd be in the middle of surgery, or eating dinner in the kitchen, or driving around at three in the morning, and suddenly they'd flash into his head – *June*, or *Annie*, or *Laura*. Names he thought he'd forgotten. Faces, once blended into one anonymous, all-encompassing girl, suddenly outlined in stark relief. His girls. The girls he'd loved.

Some of them, he knew, would never be found. Returned to the earth, transforming into mud in shallow graves, or lost in mountains of trash, arms and legs and torso a jumble in a twisted, shiny plastic bag. Most of them no one would ever miss. Except for him. He wished, so often, that just one of them could stay. But they never did, and they never could.

Hot breath slipped through knife-slash lips. He wiped sweat from his forehead with the back of a shaking wrist. His glasses had slipped down. He took them off, squinted at the smeared half-moons, and dipped them under the faucet.

A clatter at the window. A shadow hiding the moon.

He spun, eyes wide and vision blurred. Something red was slithering into the men's room, something red and brown and black.

"Whoops!" A high, delighted cackle. "Hey, sorry. Didn't know anybody was in here."

"Uh…" He fumbled for his glasses, slipped them on.

She swam into focus with fever-dream clarity. One long skinny leg cocked over the windowsill, black-booted, zipper on the side trailing up to a naked gooseflesh thigh. Scarlet mini-dress, pulled down off fragile shoulders, outlining undefined curves and tiny, plump breasts. Delicate hand gripping the window-frame, long crimson nails, perfect blood-red ovals. Waterfall of shining chestnut hair, parted in the center, cascading over one laughing brown eye. And that face, that sweet, sweet face: soft with baby fat, nose a pink pearl, lips red and glossy and rounded as a Christmas bauble. Thick chemical smell of cheap perfume, totally failing to mask her own smell, that young smell, that sugar-and-spice candy-flesh smell.

She couldn't have been more than twelve. A child. A beautiful, painted child.

He couldn't speak, could barely draw breath.

She dropped down to the dirt-slicked tiles, straightened her dress with a grimace, patted down her hair. He waited, drinking her in; sight, scent, even sound – the rustling of her clothing, the flutter of her breath.

She cast him a glance through lowered lids. Blessed him with a crooked smile. "Did I scare you? 'Cause you looked like maybe I did."

Glee in her voice. A happy trick-or-treater. *Boo! Scared ya! Scared ya!*

He knew the game. He smiled back, shook his head. "It takes more than that to scare me."

"Ooh, so you're *tough*."

Flirting. An adult game. Mimicking her elders: a hand on one hip, a flip of the hair. He smiled, didn't answer.

"Pretty rough out there tonight," she went on, eyeing him through thick lashes beaded black with mascara. "D'you know, that son of a bitch at the door wouldn't let me in? Said I didn't have enough money, even though he knows I'm good for it. Son of a bitch."

Jack cleared his throat, adjusted his glasses. "I don't suppose," He said slowly, "that your being too young might've had something to do with it?"

Quick as whiplash: "Too young for what?"

Jack was thrilled. Oh, she knew all the tricks, this one. All the clichés. She'd been well-schooled. Trained like a brightly-plumed parrot.

"Too young to hang around a club like this," he said gently.

She snorted. "Hey, that's bullshit. I got friends in here, man. I'm not some stupid kid. I do fine for myself, y'know?"

"I'm sure you do."

She raised an eyebrow, looked him over.

"Hey, listen," she said, dropping her voice, leaning closer. Jack resisted the urge to shut his eyes and breathe her in. "You're not gonna blow the whistle on me or anything, are you?"

He shook his head, placed a finger on his smiling lips. "Your secret's safe with me."

"Well, then, couldya do me a favor, maybe?" She bit her lower lip; his teeth ached in envy. "Couldya just look out the door a second, see if there's, like, any bouncers or whatever wandering around out there? Lemme know if it's safe to go in?"

"Sure." He sauntered to the door, pushed it open, peered out. Darkness beyond, thick as velvet, studded with colored lights like flashing jewels. Music almost as loud as the blood in his head.

He slipped back into the men's room. "All clear."

She grinned, clapped her red-nailed hands together. "Awesome. Thanks, Mister."

"Doctor."

Her eyes widened; he couldn't tell if she was genuinely impressed or just playing her part. "*Doctor*, huh? Ooh, wow. That's really cool."

He shrugged. "It has its moments."

"So your full name would be Doctor…?"

"Jack. Well, Kelloway. Doctor Kelloway. But call me Jack."

A Cheshire cat smile. "Doctor *Jaaaack*," she breathed, dragging it out, adding at least three more syllables. "Well, thank you, Doctor Jack. Thank you *very* much."

She brushed past him, the tips of her hair sliding over his coat sleeve. Her smell filled his nostrils, entwined itself around the coke and the music and the beating blood. Panic seized him; she was getting away, leaving his presence, leaving his life maybe, if he didn't do something right now.

"And your name would be…?" he asked.

One jewel-eye glinted in the shadow of her hair. She twirled on a too-high heel, walked backward into the darkness, head on one side. "Marty," she called, voice high as a bell. "See ya!" and she turned away, and she left him behind.

Jack watched her go, stalking into the crush of bodies on scabby, coltish legs. His heart was beating so hard his chest shook; he felt his ribs might break.

He needed her. He might die without her. Marty. This little sluttish angel who'd fallen, a gift from God, right into his lap in the middle of a stinking nightclub restroom.

Oh, yes. He was leaving with her. Tonight. No doubt about it. No choice in the matter.

He slipped from the bathroom, his eyes on her vanishing form, and began to trail after, clinging to the shadows.

He had a feeling that he would definitely remember this one. After it was all over.

Marty Sadovsky raised her face to the ceiling, felt the hot lights falling across her skin. She flung her arms out to her sides and spun in six giddy circles. She felt like laughing aloud, and did. Yeah, why the hell not? The music was so loud, no one could hear, and fuck it, she wouldn't care even if they could. She was free, she was free, she was free free *free!*

No more wandering the strip at two AM, cold and tired and hungry. No more disgusting sweaty pervs grunting over her for ten-dollar bills she was never allowed to keep for herself anyway. No more Crow. No more Crow *ever.*

She let herself sink into the music, arms over her head, flinging her hair from side to side and watching the strands burst in strobe-light flashes. She knew she should look serious, since she was here on business, but whatever – she *couldn't* contain herself, not tonight, not now that she was so happy, finally, after such a long time being just miserable as shit. It was the best night of her life, totally, one hundred per cent, and if she felt like dancing, well then, she was damn well *going* to dance and who was gonna stop her?

A sparkle of gold at the corner of her eye pulled her back into herself, reminded her why she was here; she snapped her fingers in the air, waved frantically, yelled "HEY!" at the top of her lungs. No answer; too noisy. She pushed through the crowd, laughing, dancing, spinning, and entered LaTeesha's circle that way, swinging her hips from side to side and singing, a giggle in her voice.

"Gimme things that don't last long – gimme siren, child, and do you hear at all?"

LaTeesha smiled and uncrossed her legs. "Now how on earth do *you* know the words to this song, little girl? It's older than you are."

"You always said I was an old soul, right?" Marty retorted, flopping down at LaTeesha's side and leaning her elbows on the table.

LaTeesha snorted in amusement. Apparently, Marty noted, her theme for the evening was 'gold'. A Cleopatra wig rested atop her head, strands of plastic hair threaded with gold-painted beads; her black bra top shimmered with golden sequins; her skirt, obscenely short and totally failing to disguise the bulge between her legs, shone the gold of cheap spray-paint; her long dark legs, the color and sheen of oil on water, tapered down to a pair of enormous gold platform heels. She was the least convincing drag queen Marty had ever known – and considering how unconvincing the other queens at LaTeesha's table tonight were, that was saying something – but she was beautiful. The sight of her bare arms and shoulders, more muscular than those of the bouncer outside, made Marty feel safe, protected.

Marty propped her chin on her hand and gave LaTeesha her most appealing look. "You're looking real pretty tonight, Teesh."

"Why, thank you, precious." LaTeesha gave a regal wave, sent her other friends scattering like badly-dressed birds. "So what is it you're after this fine evening?"

Marty tried to look shocked. "Who says I'm *after* anything? I didn't say I was *after* anything."

"Right. You're just here to enjoy the pleasure and the privilege of my company."

"Well, you don't have to get all *sarcastic*, Teesh. *God.*" Marty folded her arms tight and hunched her shoulders.

LaTeesha rolled her eyes. "Oh, don't do *that*. Fine, fine, your motives are pure as the driven snow. What's up with you, then, honey? Ain't seen you in, what, two whole months?"

"Yeah, that bastard Crow was, like, keeping me prisoner. I swear to God, he had me locked in the house, like, twenty-four-seven. Only let me out to work."

"Crow?"

"Savini. My pimp. I think you met him a couple times. He didn't like me hanging out with my friends."

"Pimps never do," LaTeesha said. "Don't miss that life one little bit. So how come you're out tonight, then? Crow let you off?"

"Kinda." Marty examined her nails and grinned. "I got rid of him, Teesh. He is *gone. Finito.* Out of my life for *good!*"

LaTeesha leaned back in her seat and clapped her jeweled hands together. "Outstanding, baby. Outstanding!"

"Yup." Marty waved a hand, dismissing Crow's memory with an imperious gesture. "Just walked right out and left him. Nothing he can do. I'm done with the life, Teesh. Done with the life and done with him."

"So, you going back to your parents?"

Marty spat. "Hell, no. Those fuckers? They're the ones kicked me out in the first place."

LaTeesha raised an eyebrow. "I see. I hope you're not thinking of trying to shack up with me, honey. I got enough moochers hanging offa me as it is."

"I'm not a moocher. And anyway, no, I wasn't thinking of that."

"What, then?"

"Well…"

Marty slouched in her chair, clasping her elbows. She blew a strand of hair away from her face. "Well, I guess I hadn't really thought about it yet," she said lamely. "I'll get a job, or something, maybe."

LaTeesha shot her a skeptical look. "A job? Baby, you're *twelve*."

"Thirteen next month."

LaTeesha sighed. "Can't argue with that logic. Okay, so what skills you got? Other than the kind that get you into trouble with vice, I mean."

"Ha ha. Well, I can sew." Marty turned her left palm upwards, pressed down on her index finger. "Really pretty well, actually. And, uh, I can, I can *type*, that's another thing." Ticked it off on her middle finger. "Run errands – I'm a good courier, I use to go get Crow's smack for him all the time." Ring finger. "And, um, well… you know, all sorts of stuff."

"Hm." LaTeesha tapped her nails on the tabletop. "Not the greatest resumé I've ever heard."

"Well, better than nothing. And, hey…" Marty leaned forward, lowering her voice. "Once I *do* get a job, LaTeesha, I can totally pay you back for…"

"Oh, shit, here it comes." LaTeesha sighed and rubbed her forehead.

"C'mon, Teesh," Marty whined, "you know I'm good for it. I always am. Eventually. I just need my shots, that's all."

"No can do, baby."

"*Tee-eesh!*" Marty wailed. "Come on! Why the hell not?"

LaTeesha spread her hands. "I would, baby, believe me. Only I just don't *have* any right now. Things are tough all over these days."

"But you know I need my shots," Marty insisted. Cold fingers of panic wound around her stomach, dampening the glow of her triumph. "You know I *need* them, Teesh…"

"Okay, look, don't freak out, huh? Now, you said you could

sew and run errands and shit, right?"

"Yeah, but what's that got to do with –"

"Well, there's this club on the coast. Little place, sort of an old-fashioned piano bar kinda thing, run by a couple of friends of mine, two old queens who never learned the words to any songs written after 'Over the Rainbow'. They're short-staffed, need some people to run odd jobs for them – sew some costumes here, make some coffee there. How'd you feel about leaving town?"

Marty bit down on her lip. "More than fine. I hate this fucking city."

"Great. Now, normally they wouldn't take someone your age, but I think maybe if you came with my recommendation…" LaTeesha dug into her purse, drew out a stubby eyebrow pencil, grabbed a beer-soaked cardboard coaster and began to scrawl. Marty craned her neck, trying to see if LaTeesha was writing anything especially nice about her.

LaTeesha finished and handed the coaster over. "Now, there's my rec, plus the address. Do *not* lose that. And bus fare," she added, fishing into her purse again and dropping coins into Marty's palm. "That's about the best I can do."

"What about my shots, though?"

LaTeesha crossed her arms. "Like I said, honey – I just don't got it. You'll have to hold out 'til you get to the coast. Gotta be someone there willing to sell you what you need."

"I dunno if I can wait that long." Marty rubbed her arm.

"Don't make me lose my patience, now, Marty. I've done all I can. And remember – if you get busted, I don't know anything about anything, got it?"

"Got it," Marty grumbled, pushing back her chair and standing up. "Well, thanks, Teesh," she added. She tried to squint past the darkness and the lights, tried to imprint Teesh's face upon her memory. "I appreciate it. I really do."

"No problem. Just watch yourself, baby. There's an awful lot of wolves out there."

Marty studied her nails. "Don't have to tell *me*. But I can look after myself." She looked up, smiled, and shot LaTeesha a wink. "Catch you later, then."

LaTeesha raised her arm, curled her fingers in an elegant wave. "So long, honey. You take care, now."

44

Jack's heart was convulsing, so hard he wondered briefly whether he might be suffering some sort of aneurysm. Heart attack. Quite appropriate. His heart *was* under attack, besieged, set to fire and the sword. Marty. The only way to quench the fire, to blunt the sword's sharpest edges.

She needed something. He knew that now. Listening in on her conversation with the drag queen, pressing to the wall, cocking one straining ear in her direction. His senses were so finely tuned to her already, only minutes after they'd met. Like a dog. Dog in heat. The hairs on the back of his neck prickled.

She was getting up now, exchanging more words with the man in the skirt, and drifting away to the back door. He stole after, crouching in the forest of legs and arms and torsos; managed to reach the exit first, emerging into the parking lot sweaty and rumpled. He ran shaking fingers through oil-slick hair, took off his glasses, breathed on the lenses, pushed them back on. Leaned back to wait. His breath materialized, a cold white ghost.

Puddles shimmered on black tarmac, under the sickly light of a single blue lamppost. Tire-treads formed intricate patterns in black mud underfoot. The air had the crisp, clean bite of a rainstorm. Good. She'd want to get out of the rain. His car was close.

The click of high heels. She was here, tucking something into her boot. Piece of paper. The address the drag queen had given her. Not important; she'd never get there.

She walked across the lot, whistling inexpertly, her pursed lips emitting more air than song. Her arms swung childishly at her sides, belying the sashaying suggestion in her walk; her arms said *little girl*, but her legs said *maybe more*.

He took a breath, held the cold air in his lungs, and stepped out. Careful not to look directly at her. Had to act like he was going to his car. This ridiculous pretense, this game. He loved it, and longed for it to be over.

The heels faltered, stopped. "Doctor Jack?"

He turned, plastered false surprise across his face.

"Doctor Jack, right? From the bathroom?"

"Oh! Yes, of course." As if he'd forgotten. As if he could. "And it's, uh…" He snapped his fingers twice. "Marty! Yes, Marty, isn't it?"

45

She simpered, dipped a clumsy curtsey. "That's me."

"How'd you go in there? Find your friends okay?"

"Yeah, yeah, I did…" She rubbed her long neck, cast him a long, considering look.

He waited patiently. *Ask me. I know you want drugs. I know you know I'm a doctor. Come on. Ask me, you little whore.*

"Hey, listen," she began, "Can I, uh – can I ask you for, um, for, you know, a favor, maybe?"

There. Right there.

"Um..." He shifted, adjusted his glasses. "Ah, do we really know each other well enough for that?"

"Well, uh…we *could*." She raised her eyes just enough, peeping through the lashes, and emitted a burble of sweet laughter. A spasm of want passed through Jack's body. He knew he was being manipulated, didn't care.

He leaned against a car, tilted his head. "Okay, well, just suppose you tell me what *kind* of favor you're after, and we'll see, hmm?"

She looked down, shuffled her feet. "Kind of a…medical favor."

"Oh?"

She glanced up, gaze hooded. "I need shots," she said. "Regular ones."

"Ah." He pretended not to get it. "You mean, like diabetes shots?"

"Something like that."

She wasn't looking at him any more – ashamed, perhaps – but it was too late: he'd seen the naked need in her eyes, caught the flash of hunger. An addict's greed. He loved her so completely in that moment, so totally and entirely: wanted to gnaw on her fingertips, kiss her throat hard enough to draw blood. She needed him as badly as he needed her.

"Shouldn't be a problem," he said with genuine cheer. "It's after hours, of course, but I run a clinic on the outskirts of town. If you want I can take you now and we'll see about fixing you up."

She jerked her head up. "Really?"

"Really. Come to my car."

She trotted to his side, docile and tame, now that she was close to getting what she wanted. "This is so nice of you," she offered, giving him that diamond smile.

He smiled back, and meant it. "No trouble at all."

"I can't pay."

"I understand."

She gave him a long look. "I mean I can't pay in, like, *cash*, you know?"

His smile birthed a grin. "I understand," he repeated.

She grinned back. Her arm snaked into his.

He hadn't lied. He *did* understand. Understood perfectly.

She was his now.

Marty held her lips to the window and emitted a long, slow, languid breath. Jack watched, enthralled, as she raised one fingertip and began to draw pictures in the frost.

"Better watch the road," she said, a half-smile curling her lip. She knew he was watching her, knew it and liked it. He loved her for that.

"I am," he said, enjoying the obviousness of the lie.

"Sure."

The heater hissed in comfortable silence. The car was narcotically warm, enough to put anyone to sleep. He drew the flask from his side and offered it to her. "Coffee?"

"Yeah, thanks." Marty took it, her fingers brushing his for one electric moment, and raised the flask to her lips. "Mm. S'nice."

"You must've been cold out there. That dress is pretty skimpy."

She eyeballed him. "People don't usually say they don't like it."

"I'm sure they don't. I'm just thinking of your welfare, that's all."

"I don't get welfare."

"Your wellbeing, I mean," he clarified. "Your health. You wouldn't want to catch cold."

She grinned. "Yeah. Lucky I got a doctor to help me out, huh?"

He took the flask back, pretended to take a belt from it. "How're you feeling now?" he asked.

"Now?" She settled back in her seat, closed her eyes. "Kinda sleepy," she admitted.

So she should be. There was enough Rohypnol in that coffee to put a rhinoceros into a coma.

"Want me to turn the heater off?"

"Nah." She shifted onto one exquisite hip, snuggled close. "It's nice."

He melted inside. He raised a hand tentatively – *don't spoil this moment, Jack* – and stroked the warm hair at her temple. She sighed and pressed closer. He could feel her pulse beating under his fingertips. Her life in his hand.

It didn't have to end the way it always did. Not this time. This time, with this one, it could be different. He could keep driving, drive down to Mississippi. You could get married at fourteen in Mississippi.

He could let her out. Let her out of the car, let her go on to her friends on the coast, get a job, live her life. Let her grow up.

Impossible. Oh, impossible. And yet, it was nice to dream.

"You got a wife?" Her voice drifted up from his chest. Sleepy brown eyes blinked heavily at him, as if trying hard to bring his face into focus.

He gazed down at her. "Now, if I had a wife, would I be sitting here right now with you?"

Even through the haze, she managed a sarcastic look. Made him chuckle.

"No," he admitted. "I don't have a wife." He watched the road. "Women…don't really like me."

She watched him. "Or is it that you don't really like women?"

Nick's face flickered before his eyes.

"Why'd you say that?" he asked sharply.

She shrugged.

"I'm not gay, if that's what you're thinking."

A silence. "I wasn't."

"I wouldn't be here with you if I…"

"Yeah, I believe you."

Did she? Well, it didn't matter. Soon, nothing she thought would matter.

"Here we are!" he sang, forcing the tension out of his voice as he swung the car into the clinic's driveway. The building slumbered up ahead, a long white snake, eyes blackened and dead. Frost rimed the gold plaque out front; hard drops of rain spackled white-painted bricks.

"Out you get," he murmured, supporting the sleepy girl's head on his shoulder, feeling her breath warm his cheek. He helped her out, slammed the doors shut, led her inside.

"Take off your shoes, please."

The first words he said to her as they entered the cool, clean, pristine white surgery; as he plopped her down onto the edge of the operating table; as he turned away to wash his trembling hands.

"Why?" Marty asked, voice thick and bleary, even as she started to unzip.

"I'll need you to lie on the table," Jack said, washing his hands over and over, "and your boots will scuff the surface. Besides, you're not going to need them."

"Oh. 'Kay." She kicked the boots off, curled her bare toes, and leaned back with an exhausted sigh.

He massaged his hands to quell the shaking, and strode to the cabinet. The scalpels were laid out, just as he'd left them, as he always left them: spotless and gleaming, dragon's treasure. He ran his fingers over them and picked out the third from the left, the one he liked best.

"Just lie back," he murmured. "Lie back and relax."

He ran the tip of the blade over one finger. Bright blood sprang up in its wake. He shivered at the sting of it, the biting pain. Every cell in his body screamed for release. His red tongue swept his teeth, riding the sharp canines.

"Hey…" she said thickly, glancing at his hands as he approached her, snapping on the rubber gloves. "Where'za – where'za shot? I didn't even tell you what kind…"

"Shhhh." He pressed a finger to her mouth, ran the tip over the seam where upper lip met lower. He bent lower over her, came closer, closer; he wanted to be as close as he could be, as close as anyone could be to another human being, close enough for their skin to bond, for both of them to merge.

He was on top of her now. She tried to speak but managed

49

only lost, incoherent mumbles. Her eyes rolled back, slivers of gleaming white.

"It's all right," he said. "It's really all right. Someone used to do this to me when I was your age, and I loved him a lot. So this isn't wrong. You've done this before, so you know it isn't wrong…"

He traced her lips, her cherry-tomato lips, and kissed the corner of her mouth. "You have," he whispered, "the fullest lips…"

His left hand drifted across her jawbone, brushed light fingers over her throat, laid a flattened palm on her breastbone. "The softest skin," he breathed, and pressed a kiss to her throat.

He slid down further, heart lodged in his oesophagus; he could barely breathe for the force of it. Kneeling now, kneeling before her, parting her legs with numb hands. The scalpel winked in the low light, clutched between unfeeling thumb and forefinger.

"The most beautiful…" he murmured, peeling the hem of her dress, sliding it across smooth white thigh, moving closer, closer to her, the part of her that would let him inside, the part – the part –

He stopped. Everything stopped. The blood in his veins halted; his eyes refused to see. The world went black, then white; the air turned cold and sick and foul.

Jack stared, mouth open, at the sight before him. He wasn't entirely sure what it was. Words, descriptions, had fled from him.

"What the hell is *this*?" he choked.

And that was when he happened to look up. Happened to look up into the narrowed, glittering, perfectly alert and conscious eyes of Marty Sadovsky, raised on her elbows, a vengeful young goddess whose baleful gaze devoured him whole.

"It's bigger than yours, fucker!" she spat.

She drew back her hand, faster than thought. Her nails slashed down, a crimson blur, hissing through the air.

Jack didn't feel anything at first. He wasn't sure what she'd done. He wasn't sure of anything; nothing made sense, nothing fit. He opened his mouth to ask, to plead with her to make some sense of it all. He swallowed blood.

A second mouth had opened in his throat. It would not let him speak; would not let him breathe. He hadn't realized how precious the feeling of air inside him had really been, not until now, now that he could breathe nothing but his own blood.

Marty watched him fall; her face was the image he took with

50

him on that journey through space, that endless, graceless tumble to the cold linoleum floor. As the ceiling reared up before him and the blinding glare of fluorescent light burst and seared through his optic nerves, he thought for a moment that he could taste coke on the back of his tongue; coke, yes; coke, and the sweet, salty taste of his big brother's mouth.

Marty knelt on the edge of the operating table, head cocked, watching as a halo of blood gathered around Doctor Jack's head, soaked into his white shirt. She sighed, ran a hand through her hair, and hopped down, gingerly stepping around the body.

She grabbed her boots, yanked them on and swept the zippers up. God, she must look a total mess. She pulled down her skirt and tucked her cock back between the tops of her thighs. She'd been eager to get rid of the ugly damn thing for as long as she could remember, but tonight, she felt kinda grateful to have it. It'd bought her the time she'd needed.

She dipped down to Doctor Jack, turned out his pockets, and slipped his well-stocked wallet down into her cleavage; no sense leaving all that money there for some quick-fingered coroner to grab. Besides, she'd damn well earned it.

Marty straightened up, aimed a swift kick at Jack's ribcage for good measure, stepped over him and made a beeline for the cabinets. She flung them open, tossing the contents aside, allowing glass and plastic to shatter on the floor – hey, let the cops think it'd all been a robbery, whatever. For the second time tonight, she was lucky; she found the oestrogen tablets in the second cabinet. She grabbed several jars of the little colored pills and stuffed them into a plastic bag. Sure, taking hormones in pill form wasn't as good as getting them in shots, but these would be okay for now.

She looked scornfully down at Doctor Jack. Honestly. What did he think she was, some dumbass kid? As if she hadn't learned to spot a freak a mile away by now. And, yeah, as if she'd ever take a drink from someone she didn't know. Anyway, she hated coffee.

He was just like Crow. Another wolf. Underestimating her, wanting to own her, thinking she'd do whatever he wanted, that she'd *let* him do whatever he wanted to *her*. Like she'd just roll over and play dead.

51

She wiped her fingertips on her skirt and examined her nails. Neat little trick. The razor nail. You broke off a piece of a razor blade, glued it onto one of your fingertips, painted it to look just like the rest of the nails, and you had yourself a pretty damn good little weapon.

It was the only useful thing Crow had ever taught her, the bastard. He'd have been *lucky* to have died by the razor nail, but no, the son of a bitch had to go and rape her. And then the stupid asshole had just walked away, leaving his belt right next to her on the bedpost. She hadn't known she'd had that much strength, especially not like that, naked and on fire with pain, eyes streaming black mascara – but she'd done it, she'd wrapped that belt around his neck and pulled, screaming with rage, braced against his back. And it was only when she'd dropped the belt, when he'd hit the floor, when all the fight in her was gone, that she had realized she was free. Really *free*. Not just of Crow, but of it all. No more being hit. No more being fucked. No more wolves.

She had everything she needed now. Money. Hormones. A place to go. She reached into her boot and pulled out LaTeesha's coaster, trailed her fingers over rough cardboard. There was a life out there, a real life, just waiting for her to go and grab it.

And no goddamn wolves were ever going to stand in her way again.

Young and strong and full of purpose, she threw the bag over her shoulder and strode out of the room.

Amelia Mangan *is a writer originally from London, currently living in Sydney, Australia. Her writing is featured in* Attic Toys *(ed. Jeremy C. Shipp),* Mother Goose is Dead *(eds. Michele Acker & Kirk Dougal),* The Willows Magazine, Twisted Dreams Magazine, Cthulhupalooza Magazine, *and* Akujunkan: The Infinite Process 2003 Anthology *(ed. Roseanna White), as well as the forthcoming anthologies* Blood Type *(ed. Robert S. Wilson),* Carnival of the Damned *(eds. Henry Snider & David C. Hayes) and* Women Writing the Weird II: Dreadful Daughters *(ed. Deb Hoag). She reviews books for* Good Reading Magazine*, and can be found on Twitter (@AmeliaMangan) and Facebook (facebook.com/amelia.mangan).*

PUPPYBERRIES
by John Greenwood

I was clearing out my wardrobe the other day when I came across a coat I hadn't worn in twenty years. What I found in one of the pockets reminded me of something that happened back then, when I was a different man. It hadn't crossed my mind in such a long time.

As I remember, it started one July afternoon when I was walking my daughter home from nursery school. She can't have been any more than three years old. I saw she was fiddling with something in her hand.

"Hey, Jeannie, what's that you've got?" I asked. She had a bad habit of picking up bits and pieces from the pavement.

"It's a puppyberry," she said.

"A what? Where did you get that?"

"Sadiq gave it to me," said Jeannie, holding up a roundish, brown, striated thing that fitted neatly into her little fist. I didn't know what it was. It was much too early for conkers.

"And where did Sadiq get it from?" I asked her.

She rolled her eyes and said in a sing-song voice, "Sadiq's *mummy* buyed it from the ice-cream van, and she gived it to Sadiq."

"I don't think the ice-cream van sells these," I said. "Give it here a minute, let me have a look."

Jeannie closed her fist and shoved it into her coat pocket. "But Daddy, this puppyberry is very precious and I need it for my picnic."

"I promise I'll give it you back."

Reluctantly she handed it over. "Be careful with it," she warned me.

The "puppyberry" was about the size of a large marble, coffee-coloured, rough to the touch, and covered with darker brown raised bands that reminded me of an armadillo's shell. It was warm, as though it was alive, or on second thoughts, noticing the smoky aroma, as though it had been cooked.

"So Sadiq got this from the ice-cream van?"

"No-oh," said Jeannie. "Sadiq's mummy got it from the ice-cream van."

"Right," I said, turning the hard little ball over in my hand as we wandered around the corner onto our estate.

There were three ice-cream vans operating in our neighbourhood at that time, and they all belonged to the same family. I knew this because they lived a few roads up from the school my son went to – he must have been coming up to ten. We often saw all three vans squeezed onto the one tarmac drive at the front of a terraced house with a rusting fridge-freezer on the front lawn. Years ago some amateur artist had painted them with cartoon characters who danced about holding ice-creams. But the pictures were faded and peeling, and even back then the characters were so old fashioned that I had to explain to my kids who they were: Popeye and Olive Oyl on one van, Tom and Jerry on the second, and on the third a blank-eyed, unsmiling dog even I could not identify.

They were East European, I think, or maybe Turkish or Algerian. I don't think we ever fully established where they came from. I sometimes wondered whether they were twins or triplets. There could have been two brothers or three, and you could never be sure which one you were dealing with. They all wore short white coats that were none too clean, but apart from the thick stubble on their grey chins, I could never get a good look at the faces beneath those baseball caps and hoodies. It used to annoy me that they parked their vans right outside the school gates at ten past three, so that the kids started begging for ice-cream as soon as I picked them up. "Dad," said my daughter, tugging at my sleeve. "You have to share..."

I gave her treasure back, but said, "Listen honey, you know you mustn't put this in your mouth. It's okay to play with, but it's not for eating."

My daughter pouted and crossed her arms. "Yes it is for eating. Sadiq gave it to me for my pudding, and you're a very stupid daddy."

After a while she lost interest in playing picnics with her teddies and dolls, and I slipped the thing into my pocket. When Natasha was sitting at the dining table that evening with a glass of wine, I showed her the puppyberry.

"Some kind of Indian snack?" she guessed.

"Not like any I've seen," I said. "It looks more like a seed pod. And I'm pretty sure those guys aren't Indian."

"You believe her about the ice-cream van?" said my wife.

I shrugged, and when Jeannie ran into the kitchen, her mother caught her in a big hug and sat her on her knee.

"What's this?" she asked Jeannie.

"Mummy you have snatched my puppyberry!"

"Why is it called a puppyberry?" asked Natasha, holding the little nut-brown thing out of our daughter's reach.

"Give it!"

My wife laughed. "Answer the question first!"

Jeannie assumed a teacherly expression. "To be honest, they're made by puppies, actually."

"To be honest, that sounds kind of gross, actually," said Natasha. "Here, you can have it, but do not put it in your mouth, Missy!"

That night I put it up on a high shelf in the kitchen along with the painkillers and other stuff we didn't want the kids getting their hands on, but I worried that Jeannie would see other kids putting the puppyberries in their mouths and be tempted to copy them. Trees overhung the little playground behind my daughter's nursery – had it fallen from one of these? In a spare moment I dug out an old guide to British trees. It had dozens of photos of seed pods, but nothing that resembled the puppyberry.

At that age Jeannie would latch onto a new word and use it over and over until she'd just about worn it out. We started to hear a lot about puppyberries. Her toys used them to gain magical powers. I didn't pay her much attention, and forgot all about puppyberries. But on Friday afternoons, if they had been good, our kids were allowed to choose an ice-cream or some sweets from the ice-cream van. When Friday came around, we were queuing on the pavement outside the school gates. "Have you decided what kind of ice-cream you want?" I asked Jeannie.

"I don't want an ice-cream, Daddy. I want puppyberries."

I guess I should have expected it.

"What about an ice-lolly? I'm not sure they have any puppyberries here."

I wasn't looking forward to making a fool of myself in front of the Turkish-or-whatever guy. But she's always been a girl who knows what she wants, so when we got to the front of the queue I lifted Jeannie into my arms, looked up at the unshaven, sweaty face of the ice-cream man and said, "My daughter seems to think you might have something called puppyberries? Do you know what that means?"

It took a few attempts before he understood what I was saying, but eventually he cracked a grin and said, "Puppa! Puppa? You want the puppa? Yes?"

He scooped up a handful of brown balls from a stained aluminium pan.

My daughter nodded gleefully.

"How many you want?"

I shrugged. "Enough for two little ones?"

"I give you one bag, one pound," said the ice-cream man, holding up a thick, hairy index finger.

He handed them over in a white paper bag, the kind I used to get quarters of sweets in when I was a child. It felt warm, and I said, "Careful, Jeannie, they might be hot. Let me try one first to be sure."

I took one of the puppyberries, or puppa, whatever they were, and gingerly went to take a bite. The ice-cream guy leant out of his window, wagging his finger. "No, no! Not like this. You must take off, take off," and he made a peeling gesture. Sure enough, you could pick the raised armadillo bands off with a fingernail, to reveal a creamy white sphere that had the feel of a Brazil nut only softer, or a particularly hard mushroom. I popped it into my mouth.

"You like?" asked the ice-cream man.

"Yes, very much so," I said. "They're delicious. What are they?"

"They are the puppa, yes?" said the man, which explained nothing. "Heat up, twenty minutes, not too much." He pointed to where he had set up a little two ring camping stove at the back of the van. I would have liked to have asked him more about it, but Jeannie was getting tetchy and complaining that I had stolen her treat, so we had to leave it there.

All the way home Jeannie and her big brother left a trail of peelings. I managed to save a couple of puppyberries for my wife, who always likes to try new things.

"They're good," she said. "They're delicious. They'd be good in a cake. Where does he get them from?"

"I don't know, his English is pretty crappy," I said.

"Well, try and catch his brother and find out, will you?" she said. "I bet you could make muffins with these. Or savoury scones. Have you got any more?"

The three vans may have had different pictures painted on them, but they all had the same tune. It was a strange little bar of music in a minor key, and I could never place it. Just eight melancholy notes. It sounded sort of Russian or Jewish to me – I'm not an expert. It wasn't any nursery rhyme I'd ever heard, but it stayed with me, so I could always tell when one of their vans was in the neighbourhood.

"Where do you get these things from?" I shouted, trying to make myself heard over the noise of the engine. I had to ask a couple of times before he nodded and said, "In forest, we dig. Grow under ground."

"Which forest?" I asked. "Where?"

"You know golf club? Next to golf club, little hill, many trees, many..." He groped for the right word. "...trees, like in my country, leafs very little, thin. You dig, then wash, then cook, just twenty minutes, no more."

I nodded – I knew of a copse on a hillock next to the golf course. It was where my mates and I used to go to drink when we were seventeen.

I wanted to ask him more about the trees, and about what country he and his brothers came from, but by this time there was a queue behind us. We walked in the park that evening, and didn't go home until the day's heat had faded and our shadows stretched out before us like giants. The good weather had finally arrived. We spent that whole summer outdoors, barbequing in the back garden, playing football in the park, watching the kids grow in strength and confidence. Thinking back, I can almost smell those puppyberries.

Everyone in the family took to them, even Ryan, who was such a fussy eater. I remember one Sunday afternoon in the park, a boy coming down the hill towards us on his bike, going much too fast. We all froze, and at the very last second the boy – he must have been twelve or so – swerved, missing my son by an inch. It was clear to me he had done it deliberately. Normally Ryan would have let it go – he didn't like confrontations. But this time, when the older boy did a U-turn at the park gates my son calmly picked up a branch from the side of the path. As the bike passed him, very fast and close again, he crouched down and in one smooth motion shoved the stick between the spokes of the back wheel. The bike skidded onto its side and the boy went sprawling on the tarmac, clutching a grazed knee. He hobbled off, pushing his bike and angrily wiping away tears. It's silly I know, but even though it happened two decades ago, I can't recall that incident without a little swell of pride.

I told my wife that story later and she laughed. That summer was also when things started improving between me and her. Those early years with the kids had been hard going for us both. She worked long hours and we didn't see much of one another. When the thaw came, we were both surprised. It felt like coming out of hibernation. I don't know what happened exactly – Jeannie's asthma had cleared up unexpectedly, and Ryan was really coming out of his shell. I suppose there was just less to worry about. The future looked pretty good.

We called them berries but nobody could say for sure what they were. Somebody swore they were a kind of shellfish from Sri Lanka; quite a few people considered them a type of mushroom; our neighbour Mike said his father had seen something similar hanging from a tree in his local botanical gardens. The one thing they didn't look like were berries. I guess we had the children to blame for that misnomer. I always thought the most likely explanation was that they were related to the truffle. After all, the ice-cream guy had said that he dug them up in the forest.

There was one weekend we decided to go for a family walk out to that little hill by the golf course. I took a couple of trowels and a plastic bag, hoping we could find some puppyberries for ourselves. The kids, God bless them, were as enthusiastic as I was and ran around between the pine trees, shoving their little beach spades between the roots, but we really didn't know what we were looking for, and I felt a little foolish. It was dispiriting too to see what had happened to that bit of green space. There were dozens of empty cider bottles, cigarette packets and used condoms strewn amidst the pine needles. When Natasha found a hypodermic we told the kids to give over looking for puppyberries, and we all climbed up to where the hill emerged from the trees to give a bit of a view over the golf course, the park and the school. We couldn't quite make out our house, but Jeannie swore she could see it. It was a shame about all the litter.

I remember that day because of something Ryan said to me. We were sitting eating our sandwiches when out of nowhere he said, "Dad, one day I'm going to make you proud of me."

I said, "Son, I'm already proud of you. I'm proud of both you kids. You make me proud every day."

"I know that," he said. "But one day I'm going to do something big, and then you'll be even prouder."

I put my arm around his shoulder. "What kind of big thing are we talking about?"

"You'll see," was all he would tell me.

What more could a father ask of his son? It more than made up for any bitterness I felt at failing to dig up any puppyberries.

The next time the ice-cream van pulled up on the estate, I told the driver about our failed attempt to dig for puppyberries. For a moment he looked down at me blankly, and I wondered whether he was going to be angry that we'd trespassed on his turf. When he finally understood, he said, "No, no, you need the dog for this."

"Oh? Your brother – was it your brother I spoke to last time? – never said anything about a dog."

"Yes, yes. Special dog, very clever dog."

The man did a clumsy imitation of a dog snuffling in the undergrowth, and the children laughed. The man held up a greasy old supermarket carrier bag that bulged with many hundreds of berries.

"My brother, he find a new place, look! Many, many puppa. Extra-large!" he said with a yellow grin.

He pulled out a handful and showed us – raw, the berries were a lustrous green, like a large, armoured caterpillar that had rolled itself into a ball.

I opened my wallet. "I'll take ten bags," I said. "Do you have a bulk rate?"

The man shook his head slowly. "Six maximum," he said, "Same for everyone." There was no malice in his tone, but he was not to be shifted. We made do with six bags.

At least the vans were doing the rounds every day, seven days a week, and the brothers never seemed to run out of puppa. By the start of the next school year we were eating them three meals a day – sprinkled on muesli or cereal at breakfast; ground up into a paté to spread on sandwiches for lunch; roasted or stuffed into a chicken at dinnertime. There were endless variations. Every morning, even before the milkman had come, we looked forward to hearing that funny old klezmer melody ringing out.

We expected a bit of grousing from the kids at the start of a new academic year – having to dig their old school uniforms out of the wardrobe after six weeks of freedom – but that year they were both raring to go. Ryan had a new teacher who'd just started at the school, Mrs Booth, and at first he seemed to get along with her pretty well. She was a small, pale, softly-spoken woman in her fifties, and from what I heard in the schoolyard, an experienced teacher. I never found out why she had moved jobs to our school. Here was a single, middle-aged woman moving into a junior position in a new school when she was already coming towards the end of her career – well, if Natasha and I had been more on the ball perhaps that fact alone would have set alarm bells ringing.

We only began to understand Mrs Booth's character flaws when she confiscated some of the puppyberries we'd put in Ryan's pockets to take into class. He tended to get peckish around mid-morning, and this seemed like a natural solution. No doubt other kids from our estate had them hidden away in their pockets and desk drawers too, but it was Ryan who Mrs Booth pounced on. Our boy had never been in trouble before in his life, and we had always brought him up to tell the truth, so when his new teacher asked him where he'd got them from, he told her straight away about the ice-cream vans. That afternoon at going-home time I found a tart little note in Ryan's schoolbag asking us not to send our children to school with snacks – fruit and milk would be provided by the school. I didn't pay a great deal of attention to this, although I do recall Ryan complaining at the unfairness of it, and I had to agree with him. But my heckles were well and truly up that Friday, when all the parents were handed a letter on the school's headed paper, signed by both Mrs Booth and, if it can be believed, the Head teacher, whose opinion I had always respected.

It had come to Mrs Booth's attention, the letter began, that certain ice-cream vans in the area had been selling an unidentified type of mushroom or nut to some of the children outside the school gates. While the school was not responsible for the actions of pupils outside school hours, it had a duty of care, and until the safety of the product could be guaranteed, the school had no option but to ban these vendors from operating on or around the school's property.

"They can't do it," said Natasha, who worked as a paralegal and understood more than I did about such things. "They have no jurisdiction over the roads surrounding the school, let alone on the estate. Just let that Mrs Booth come up here and try to stop us. And if it's just a matter of cleaning the vans up a bit, we can give them a bit of a push in that direction, can't we? Hell, I'll even put their aprons through the wash myself if it means proving this stupid woman wrong."

We both knew that wouldn't be the end of it. If I knew anything about the local authorities, the idea of two guys with dogs digging up berries in a forest and selling them to schoolchildren was guaranteed to cause ructions. Of course, we could see with our own eyes just how nutritious the puppyberries were: our kids were taller, smarter and tougher than most of their peers, and the kids from our estate were getting a bit of a reputation as the ones to watch. I had even overheard my son in the schoolyard telling another boy, "Well, you're not from our street, but I suppose I can be friends with you, just for today though." They were doing us proud, and I had no doubt that those berries had something to do with it. It was like Omega 3 oils or antioxidants – something was supercharging their brains. Only the most pig-headed would try and toss a spanner in. But by her actions, Mrs Booth had proven herself an unworthy teacher.

I talked it over with Mike. We could hardly complain about her to the Head teacher – somehow she'd bamboozled that kindly old man into backing her up on this misguided campaign. And we all knew that the school governors would side with him in a dispute. Mike was all for confronting the woman and arguing it out, but I said to him, "Mike, you haven't met this woman. I have. If we go in there with all guns blazing she's only going to harden her position. You've read the letter yourself – this is not a reasonable human being we're dealing with here."

I don't recall that as one of the happiest weekends our family ever spent together. Natasha and I got sick of going over the same old ground. What if they really did shut down the ice-cream vans? We tried our best to keep the facts from the kids, but we were both tetchy and uptight and kids are sensitive to things. If this Booth woman really did follow through on her threat, of course they would have to know. But how do you tell your four year old daughter something like that?

In the end, it was Ryan who came up with the solution. He appeared in the doorway to my study when I was researching online about which breeds of dog were good for truffle-hunting.

"This thing about Mrs Booth..." he started.

He had a look about him that startled me. Something in his solid stance, or his level gaze, told me that he had changed. Perhaps it was just that he was growing up.

"What about her?" I said.

"I think you had better leave it to us."

"And who is this *us*?"

His mouth was set, determined to see it through.

"Me and some of the other boys from the estate," he said. "The ones who've been eating the berries."

"Ah?"

"You know, it's not difficult to find out where somebody lives. Like a teacher."

I nodded. "Just what is it that you plan to do?"

"I think it's best that we don't discuss it. The real question is: how much do you trust me?"

I looked at his earnest face without, I hope, a hint of condescension in mine. I knew I had to answer him without hesitation or I was lost.

"Completely and without question."

"Then there's nothing else to discuss," he said.

As he was about to leave the room, I called him back. "Is there anything I can do to help? Anything you need from me? Money? Equipment?"

Still business-like, he shook his head. "I don't think so, Dad," he replied. "But thank you for offering."

They had to go through the usual police investigation, but nothing was ever proved. My son has always had a meticulous personality, and even back then, when he set out to do a job, he did it properly. One of Mike's brothers was on the local constabulary, so that helped to smooth things over. It was as though Mrs Booth had just walked out of her flat one evening and never returned. And for all I know, perhaps that is just what happened.

Some of the other parents expressed their shock, but I took the line that our children were better off without a psychologically unstable teacher. Her recent actions over the business of the puppyberries – the sheer vindictiveness of it – had proven this. As for the Head teacher, he had hardly done himself credit in appointing her, but he was approaching retirement, and at his age could be forgiven for allowing himself to be bullied by an assertive newcomer.

Life looked set to continue its smooth course, and in this we were mistaken. As the autumn wore on, the ice-cream vans stopped coming round so regularly, then abruptly ceased trading. The three rusting vans with their badly copied cartoon characters were no longer parked on the drive where we had got used to seeing them. Many times (including once in the dead of night) we went to hammer on their door and peer through the ragged curtains in the front window, but there was no sign of anyone living there. The rusting fridge-freezer in the front garden had been joined by an old settee which, over the course of that autumn and winter, rotted down to a steel frame and springs and countless fragments of industrial foam which the wind teased into eddies around the school playground and surrounding streets. There was a rumour that Mike's three boys broke into the house, but there were no puppyberries to be found. All they found was the rotted cadaver of a dog. Years later Mike told me that it was no dog, it was something else. But by that point he was in a bad way with the drink, and not making a lot of sense.

It was a hard time for everyone. Different families on the estate coped in different ways. Some hoarded the few remaining berries they had and eked them out a few slivers at a time. I wasted a lot of money on a sniffer dog, and made many visits to the little wooded area behind the golf course. We found nothing and Natasha persuaded me to have the dog put down. I expected this to upset Ryan and Jeannie, but they were indifferent to it. As a matter of fact they suffered less from the absence of puppyberries than their parents. I recall that winter as one long, gnawing hunger without hope of respite, but for the children, all those children growing up round by us on the estate, the summer of puppyberries was just one stage in life they had moved on from.

The one thing that made it easier for us to bear was watching Ryan and Jeannie growing so strong and determined. They learned early that you must never let anybody stand in your way. They've done well for themselves and have never been a worry to us, which is as much as any parent can reasonably ask. There was a bit of fuss at Ryan's university when an unattractive girl made some trumped-up allegations, but he straightened it all out in his own inimitable way. He's got his bar exams next month, and I have no doubt he'll sail through. And Jeannie's been no slouch either – she's hoping to be selected as the Party candidate in next year's general election. By sheer coincidence one of Mike's kids – I say kids, but he's now a father of three with a receding hairline – is already an MP, and Jeannie tells us he's been ever so helpful. Not so helpful are a gaggle of activists who have been mounting a campaign to get my daughter thrown out of the Party. But if I know Jeannie, she won't let the Mrs Booths of this world keep her down. Ryan's promised to give her all the help he can. It's a funny thing, but a lot of the kids from our estate have really taken the world by the scruff of its neck. Jeannie and Ryan are still in touch with some of them. They've got very bright futures ahead of them, not that we ever doubted it for a moment back when we used to wander out of the house of a summer evening, hand in hand, to meet the ice-cream van.

Like I say, that all happened two decades ago, though I can sometimes barely believe it myself. And to tell the truth, I've hardly thought about those puppyberries since. Sometimes when the kitchen radio tunes out, I can hear that little eastern melody, just audible, playing somewhere behind the white noise, a long way off. Like a message, but not for me. And sometimes, when I'm on my own, putting out the bins or working on my little projects in the garage, I wonder what Ryan and Jeannie are getting up to, and find myself shaking and crying with fear, though I can't for the life of me think why. We're getting old, as Natasha reminds me. I've played my part. It's time for the next generation to take the stage. I try to find comfort in that.

That puppyberry must have lain undisturbed in my coat pocket all these years. When I held that little brown ball in my hand, I experienced a little stab of joy, like going to meet an old friend. But it was gone in a moment: on closer inspection I could see that it was hollow, just a brittle shell with a neat, round hole in one side, as though something had burrowed its way out.

John Greenwood *is the co-editor of* Theaker's Quarterly Fiction, *where most of his previously published writing can be found online. His major influences are books he has heard of but may never get round to reading. He works as a bookseller and lives in Birmingham. He has two entirely normal children.*

LIKE CLOCKWORK
by Benedict J. Jones

A cog turns, gears click, discs spin and it is as though my whole world has fallen into place. I watch as the parts move in their peculiar mechanical way and then I remember to breathe. I feel like I have managed to reach inside my own mind and turn a dream of smoke into the tangible form that lies on the bench in front of me. My hands run over the hard moving parts, as if I am daring them to vanish back to mist beneath my fingers.

The room is dark except for a few lamps and the shadows flex and roll as the machinery continues its cycle. I close my eyes and let the beautiful click-click rhythm fill my head. When I open my eyes again I do not know how much time has passed. I have never felt such peace. But my dream is not complete. I let myself touch, once again, the naked brass and steel and I shiver with pleasure at the thought of the finished article.

Outside the sun's light is harsh even though the morning is cold. Dirty snow lines the gutters and I throw my hood up against the brightness. As early as it is the usual shower of drunks has already begun to congregate around the benches on the parade; missing teeth, rheumy eyes, unwashed coats and cans of super strength amnesiac. I cross the square to avoid their animal chatter. The noises of the city around me seem at odds with the machine song which is still turning circles in my mind. I begin to tap my fingernails against the blade of the knife in my pocket in an attempt to mimic the click-click tattoo in my head. The queue at the bus stop makes bile rise in my throat so I pound my way across the concrete and try to think good thoughts.

I cut away from the main road and stab into the alleys and backstreets. As I walk the forgotten web of grey places it becomes easy, for a few minutes at least, to believe that I am utterly alone and my breathing slows to mirror the click-click of the gears and cogs that echoes in my ears. My calm is short lived. The boom-boom of a car's sound system drowns out the rhythm in my mind and shatters my peace. I stop and press my forehead against the rough brick wall of a building. I can feel the bass from the car through the brick and I continue to press until the sound recedes and my forehead is left raw. Then I turn and carry on into the depths of the back streets.

My heart now beats out of time with the clockwork rotations of my dream. I stop. I stare. Through the window of a dry cleaners I catch a glimpse of a nest of dark hair that has hooked my eyes, dark, dark hair that reminds me of Caitlin O'Reerdon; my first love, hair the colour of unmilked coffee and eyes like storm clouds. I would stare at her hair for hours, sit behind her in class and try to hold the smell of it in my nose until I could remember it in my dreams. Then the memory comes of the day I couldn't help myself, the day that I tried to trim a lock of her hair, the teacher catching me, detention and then Leon Carver splitting my lip and leaving me on the floor at the school gates. I just watched Caitlin after that, from beneath hooded lids, from across the playground or the other side of the classroom. Mum was still in chemo then, broken. The summer came and then afterwards Caitlin went to an all-girls school and I was shipped off to the local mixed comprehensive. Mum had died in the second week of the holidays. I close my eyes and try to remember the smell of Caitlin's hair. I don't open them until I stumble off the kerb further down the street.

I'm breathing too hard, too fast, and I begin to run, trying to outpace the dreams of the past. I run and I run and I run, through the door to the flats, past the lift and up the stairs. I take the steps two at a time and soon the muscles in my legs burn. Through the front I go and into the cave-like darkness of the flat beyond, my heart fluttering in my chest like a bird trapped in a cage of bones. It only begins to slow when I caress the gears and cogs and run my fingers over the rods and wires. I leave the lamps off and lay down on the sofa. The rhythm of the machine returns and sleep comes easy.

When I awake the darkness clings to me like a shroud and my breathing is slow and even. I gulp water greedily from the tap and then take to the streets again. The city never sleeps, it merely dozes, but within that dozing, as I walk, I can feel some semblance of freedom. I roam the orange lit back streets and deserted side roads like an urban fox on the hunt for scraps. I scale a chain-link fence and follow the tracks into the tube tunnels and I completely escape the confines of the streets and boulevards.

My Dad couldn't be there for me, I realise that now, my

Mum had kept him grounded and without her anchorage he floated, lost, in a world of booze, bookies and melancholy. One Saturday morning my Granddad turned up, packed a bag of my things, sat me in his car and had a talk with Dad. At the end of the talk I left with Granddad and never saw my father again.

As I walk the tracks I think of secondary school and my second love. I saw her on the first day and for weeks could think of nothing but the terrain of her face; the rounded hills of her cheekbones, the peak of her soft nose and the bow curve of her lips. Her name was Yaz Hasan and I spent hours attempting to map her features in a sketchbook. But no matter how many times I drew and redrew her face I could never quite capture the essence of the beauty I saw in it. It would have been okay if I had just stuck with the drawing but my frustration with my inability to trap her face on a page made me borrow Granddad's camera and keep it in the pocket of my blazer until I saw my chance. Yaz had noticed me watching and seen me sketching and she normally just gave a shy smile and looked away. I tried to be discreet when I snapped a picture of her but she saw, she saw and her friends saw and her cousin Ozzie saw. They caught me in the toilets after school; Ozzie his brother Sam and two of their friends. When they left Granddad's camera was splintered and crushed, there was blood on the floor and my piss was rusty for a week. My heart was broken and that hurt more than the beating or the punishments when Granddad found out about his camera. I had no friends so I spent more and more time with Granddad in his shop. I watched over his shoulder as he fiddled and tinkered with watches and clocks.

"Treat them right and they're more reliable than people." He would tell me. I smile as I remember Granddad's words.

I began working with Granddad and he soon saw that I was willing and more than able. It made him smile. My own father, long since found hanging in a cheap hotel, had taken no intricacies of the trade but I wanted to know it all – what made things work in the way in which they did. And that in turn led to other problems. The neighbours caught me with their dog, a bad tempered mongrel that barked at me whenever I passed. If you could fix a broken watch by getting at the insides then why not an animal? I know now that I was wrong, animals are what they are – unreliable. They cannot be fixed. Granddad tried but I was sent away to the special school.

The others that I found there were much worse than me – I had tried to fix something whereas all they knew was how to break and destroy. But there I found my third love – Siobhan Lacey. Her legs moved with the grace of predators I had seen in nature films. When I waited for sleep in my room, which I thought of as a cell, all I could think about was the slim grandeur of the muscles in those legs and how they made her arse sway as she walked. I watched but did not act. The past had taught me what happened when I made a wrong move. I was learning, the special school was teaching me to be sly. I watched Siobhan and studied her habits. Siobhan Lacey was a drug and alcohol abuser who had been caught in the passenger seat of a stolen car after a homeless man was burnt three quarters to death. My Granddad sent me money and other things to make my life easier so I swapped, traded and bought the things I needed. The odd half bottle of cheap vodka, ten wrap of chocolate coloured cannabis resin or packet of cigarettes and she would let me run my hands up her legs from her ankles, over her thighs, to the arse that lay above. I came as I touched her. For a few weeks I was in heaven. But like all things heaven has its limits and time was one of them. I was released back into Granddad's care, and for a while I thought about getting myself sent back so that I could be with her, but then I lost myself in working at the shop.

When I emerge from the tube tunnels the night sky stretches above me like a dark protective parasol. In the distance I can see the first light of the day and so I lift my feet and trudge back towards the flat, spent from my nocturnal walk. When I get back I keep the curtains drawn and tinker with my creation – oil the gears, smooth the motion. My body demands sleep but my mind is a cruel taskmaster. I try to remember the last time I ate but I can't. When I peek out through the curtains I see that the snow is falling again. I cannot see anyone else out on the expanse of the estate. I smile and collect my tools. My feet crunch across the snow and fragments of bodies like chopped up photographs fill my mind; Caitlin, Granddad, Yaz, my mother, Siobhan, my father and all the others.

I was in prison when Granddad died; they wouldn't let me out for the funeral. I first met Shelly Lennox when she came into the shop to have her watch fixed. As Granddad's health had failed it fell to me to run the shop. The sun was bright and harsh the day she came in and a headache had been gnawing at my nerves all morning.

When she passed me her watch my eyes touched on her hands; the perfect shape of each finger in relation to the next only spoilt by the engagement band around one finger. I found it hard to swallow and I could not look her in the eye as I took down her details – name, phone number, address… Three weeks later the police caught me in her flat, her bedroom. I had only gone to take a pair of her gloves but when I saw her hand atop the duvet I could not help but stroke the backs of her fingers. A neighbour had seen me go in through the bathroom window. Shelly awoke as the police arrived. The knife in my pocket added a year to my sentence. I only served nineteen months but they were a hard year and a half; spit in my dinner, boiling margarine thrown at me and a beating that had me pissing blood for a week. When I got out Granddad was dead and the shop was gone. Prison gave me time though, time to think and time to plan. I thought about my loves from over the years and I began to plan.

The house is silent when I enter. Special school and prison taught me a lot. I hear someone upstairs and I move towards the sound. The bathroom door is open and the light is on. A man stands pissing into the toilet, his relief audible. In one movement I pull his head back and cut his throat. I lay him down softly on the floor and turn out the light before heading to the bedroom. Soft snores from beneath the sheets draw me nearer. I must make more noise than I think because she sits up and tries to blink the sleep from her dark eyes.

"Hello, Yaz. Don't worry, hon, I only need your face."

Back in the flat now. Tired, oh so tired. So much done, work finished but I feel like I have a lifetime of sleep calling to me. Slide the key in, turn the key, and wind you up. I can hear them now, outside on the estate like villagers of old psyching themselves up to break into the monster's castle. The police won't be here for hours. No pitchforks and flaming torches out there; hammers, golf clubs, knives and bottles of petrol. The key turns quicker now, easier, because I'm eager to hear you click-click rhythm. I can hear the hands banging at the door. The locks will hold, for now at least. You stand, your arm rises and you offer me your/Shelly's hand and I look up into you/Yaz's eyes and I smile. You draw me into your embrace and I

70

smell your/Caitlin's hair. You move well on your/Siobhan's legs and we dance around the clutter of the front room to the music of your cogs and gears. The front door collapses and they flood the flat. The hammering starts on the front room door and I know it won't be long now. Finally I have you and now they have come to take you from me. Still, time for one last dance and you are willing, reliable, just like clockwork always is.

Benedict J Jones *is a writer of short crime and horror stories, although he occasionally wanders into the worlds of victoriana and the western. He lives in South East London and has been having his work published in the small presses since 2008 with appearances in* Out of the Gutter, Big Pulp!, Encounters Magazine, the Western Online, Delivered Magazine, Penpusher Magazine, *and on many websites. His stories have also appeared in anthologies from Dark Minds Press and Full Dark City Press. He can be found online at benedictjjones.webs.com.*

SPECIAL GIRL
by E.M. Salter

They've had others with them a few times over the years. Weeping little girls, some around her own age, some younger, all of them stupid idiots who begged for them to stop and didn't realise how lucky they were. How special. *Chosen.*

But she's the only one who gets to stay after the other girls have gone silent. When her daddy gets back from his long drives with an empty car and weary eyes, he always scrubs a hand over his face and climbs into bed beside her. Always the bed creaks as the darkness is filled with whispered instructions that are never needed. Always, she knows what to do.

She screws up her eyes as unbidden tears leak out, pain stabbing in her gut, but his hands on her face and her body make her feel safe. She's the one who gets to stay. She's the one he needs.

She was seven years old when he took her in. Her first dad had lost his job three months earlier and her parents couldn't afford to look after her anymore, he told her. She had two sisters, and three girls were expensive, he said, so they had to choose which one they loved the least and wanted to get rid of. It was hard for them but her parents had told him about the tantrum she'd thrown a week ago at the school gates. She couldn't remember now what it was about but that had been the last straw for them. They knew they'd be better off without her.

"They were very disappointed in you," he told her. "So ungrateful, behaving like a spoiled little brat. I don't blame them for giving you away."

She'd sobbed loudly, insisted it wasn't true, felt so scared and more alone than she'd ever thought possible. He'd scooped her up into a hug that was too tight and whispered soothingly into her hair.

"It's okay," he said, rubbing circles over her back. "I'm giving you another chance. I'm not going to get rid of you like they did. I'll be your daddy now. Just promise me you'll be a good girl from now on and I'll never leave you alone."

She's had many names over the years; a new one for each city or town they moved to. Hannah, Katie, Louise. After a while he let her choose her own name. Ariel, Miley, Hermione. She keeps a list of possibilities in a spiral-bound notebook and whenever she adds to it her daddy chuckles and ruffles her hair.

At least... he used to. He's been smiling at her and touching her less and less, though she doesn't realise it until one day when he's watching her get dressed.

"You're growing out of those clothes," he says.

His face is bland as he says it and there is no admonishment in his voice, but something about his tone makes her cross her arms across her chest, ashamed, hiding the place where her pink t-shirt is tight and straining.

She tries to find baggier clothes but she doesn't have any. She tries to eat less, thinking that might help, but it doesn't work.

Then one day he brings home fish and chips for dinner and while he squirts ketchup onto his plate he tells her there's another girl. A girl like her. A girl whose parents can't afford to keep her so they've asked him to take care of her.

"She'll probably be scared, like you were, but you'll help her understand, won't you?" he says.

She feels sick. She wants to scream and throw things and make him love her again. She stares at her chips and suddenly they are the most unappetising thing she's ever seen, but somehow she manages to stitch a smile to her face.

"Of course I will," she says lightly. She gets up, walks round the table to where he's sitting and wraps her arms around his neck. He smiles but she feels him flinch when her chest presses against his back.

"Finish your dinner," he says, patting her hand.

Usually he lets her help choose. It's only fair if she gets to play with

73

them as well, he says. But with this new girl she gets no say. She's just there, eating a chocolate bar and asking when her mum will come and pick her up.

"Why don't you come with me, sweetheart," he says, with a smile she hasn't seen in too long. "We should have a little chat."

He takes the girl into the bedroom and it doesn't take long before she's crying. The wailing penetrates the air, barely muffled by the door that's shutting them in and shutting her out.

She sits on the bathroom floor and listens to the girl's cries. Pain and anger and fear; she knows exactly what is happening and suddenly it hits her that she won't ever have to go through that again. She won't ever feel that stabbing pain, or have to keep from choking. She won't ever be needed like that again.

She waits for what feels like hours for the wailing to subside, then hesitates until she hears her daddy's footsteps walking down the hall.

She opens the bedroom door gently. The small girl is huddled on the bed, cocooned by rumpled sheets.

"What's your name?" she says, gingerly kneeling next to the bed, forcing herself into the girl's eye line.

The girl's voice is choked and thin. "Chloe."

"I'm Amy." It's the first time she's said her real name in eight years. The soft syllable feels wrong in her mouth and the sound of it is jarring. "I know you don't want to be here," she says softly. "I know how scared you are. But if you don't show it then he won't hurt you again. Can you do that? Can you be brave for me?"

The girl looks at her with watery eyes but doesn't say anything.

Gently, Amy slides onto the bed. The girl flinches but doesn't make a sound, even when Amy reaches out and takes a pillow from behind her.

"Can you be brave?" Amy says again.

The girl starts to cry again but doesn't fight back when the pillow comes down over her face. Amy puts all her strength into it anyway, climbing on top of the girl and straining with the effort.

"He's mine," she hisses. "Not yours. Not anyone's. *I'm* the one he needs."

She releases the pillow when she feels the girl go perfectly still.

"I'm his special girl."

Emily Salter graduated from the University of Manchester in 2006 with a degree in Film Studies, Literary Studies and Drama. As awesome as it was to spend three years watching films and reading books, it hasn't been of much practical use to her. Her various jobs have included legal secretary, casting assistant, chugger, Christmas Elf and giant snowman. In between being an occasional actress she is working on a YA sci-fi novel. She has previously been published in Pulp Idol *(SFX/Gollancz 2006) and* Time Well Bent *(Lethe Press, 2009), and is one of the writers of the forthcoming crowd-sourced feature film* 50 Kisses. *Originally from Northampton, she now lives in Manchester with her boyfriend and other animals. Emily can be found on Twitter @emilysomeday.*

FIVE AN HOUR
by Devan Goldstein

My first day on the butterscotch line, they tell me I can eat five chews an hour.

Frank says, "That's more than on the taffy line." Frank works across from me. He and I box the butterscotches, fifty a box.

"If they're so worried about money," I ask, "why do they let us eat the candy at all?"

Frank throws ten or fifteen pieces into a box. Then he asks me if I know Kevin Mercer.

"No."

"Kevin worked here for three months. Left a year ago, I guess, and opened up the hot dog stand outside. Know why he quit?"

"No."

"Never ate the candy. Without the candy, this job sucks."

I wonder how much worse this job could be than the one he has now. "I guess he eats the hot dogs," I say.

My second week on the job, I start to make rules to pace myself. I've been throwing two or three butterscotches into my mouth at the top of each hour, and the long stretches after my rations run out have been murder. As the candy goes by on the line, it talks to every part of you: your hands, your nose, your soul.

The first rule I make is, one piece at a time. Last Friday, I told Frank I've got a big mouth, and he said, "If a whale worked the line, he'd get five an hour just like you. You think he'd bitch about his big mouth?"

I didn't know if whales bitched, I told him, but did he have to be so rude?

The second rule is, stick to some kind of schedule. At first, I think I should have one butterscotch every twelve minutes. But then I think of Swagger, and how slow the strippers there unwrap themselves, the good ones anyway, and make you wait for it. So

76

maybe I'll have one piece at the one-minute mark, then wait for at the half-hour, then one every ten minutes for the rest of the hour.

I ask Frank which system he thinks will work better.

"I just eat them when I eat them," Frank says. "But everybody's different."

"You must have seen guys try different ways, though. Who's worked here the longest?"

Frank looks at me like I just dumped his box of butterscotches onto the floor, and then says, "I have."

By the end of my third week, I have tried five different schedules, and even messed around with eating two pieces at a time again. But the problem isn't the schedule. It's the candies. Too many of them go by. It just makes you want endless chewy butterscotch.

On a break, I tell these things to Marcus, the floor manager. Then I ask him: What if somebody sent the butterscotch rations down the caramel line, instead, and the taffy down the butterscotch line, and the caramel down the taffy line? That way, we'd all get excited when the candies we could eat came by, but we wouldn't care about the ones we were cutting or wrapping or boxing. We could store up candies, too, like a bank account.

"A bank account," Marcus says. Then he tells me to go get a hot dog.

"I hate hot dogs," I say.

"Then just eat the bun," he says, and I do, wishing he'd listen to my idea like I listened to his.

Over the next few days, I bring in different things to chew on in between pieces of candy. I like the springiness of balloons, but Frank complains about how loud they squeak between my teeth. A piece of my old brown belt makes less noise, but the leather makes my tongue sting by lunchtime. Silly Putty disintegrates in ten minutes, and I pick it out from the spaces around my teeth for the rest of the day. I probably swallow half of it down with my butterscotch rations.

And anyway, nothing replaces the candy, nothing makes me want it less, not even for the ten minutes between late-in-the-hour butterscotches.

Frank and I hardly talk anymore, but one day I ask him, "You ever try quitting the candy?"

He says, "This job sucks without the candy. Only reason to quit the candy is to quit the job."

I know he's right. You can't quit the candy.

Soon, I start to think about the candy in a different way. I imagine naked fat women swimming through grain silos full of butterscotches. I think of my grandfather's anal medicine, and I wonder if stuffing butterscotches up my ass would keep me from wanting them so bad, or if they have to hit your taste buds to work.

Then, I have an idea: I could easily fill two boxes at a time, one box with my left hand, and one with my right, switching every so often to make up for the difference in speed between my two hands. If I can fill two boxes, I should get double rations.

The next morning, I wait in the parking lot to tell Frank my idea.

When he opens his car door, I say, "I could fill two boxes at a time, and get double rations."

Frank looks at me the way Marcus did when he told me to eat a hot dog bun. Then he starts to walk away.

"Where are you going?" I ask.

"Inside," he says. "so I can do my job and then go back home."

I walk after him, and put my hand on his shoulder. "Frank, wait."

As he brushes my hand away, I notice how bony his shoulder feels, like I could crumble it in my hand. And if I did, he couldn't work the butterscotch line anymore. Marcus would have no choice but to ask me to fill two boxes at a time.

Then I grab the collar of his jacket and pull it hard. Frank falls onto the pavement. He looks up at me, and where his eyes usually are I see two unwrapped butterscotches. As I reach for the one on the right, I think, if he has one butterscotch in each eye, his head must be full of them.

Devan Goldstein's *writing has appeared in* The Collagist, The Rumpus, A List Apart, *and elsewhere. He lives in Pittsburgh, Pennsylvania, with his wife and son, and works as a web usability and strategy consultant.*

BRED IN THE BONE
by Jeff Gardiner

I can't complain about my childhood. I had everything a kid could need: toys, my own room, food, a regular routine and I could watch the TV as much as I wanted. The only thing I felt some regret about my parents being too strict about me seeing friends, but they had their reasons and I understood them too.

To be honest I didn't have many friends anyway, only Robbo at school and we got into some trouble together, although I was scared of doing anything too bad as it only upset my parents and you don't want to know my Dad when he's angry. Me and Robbo were never bullies or anything like that, just a bit naughty – you know; lazy, not bothering to do the work properly, losing books, giggling and chatting – the sort of things that really irritate teachers, but never get you into serious trouble. We bunked as well, but were clever about it and could expertly forge absence notes. Our form tutor never seemed unduly bothered. I never told my teachers anything, I just kept quiet at school and everyone left me to get on with my own thing.

After each day at school, I'd walk home, as it's only a couple of miles, and go to the chip shop for our regular family order. I usually got home about five and I'd have to tidy up the place – usually the mess left by my Dad – feed the dog, a bull terrier called Trooper, and then when Mum came home at six she'd stick the dinner in the microwave and I'd go and wake up Dad.

Dad could be a bit unpredictable at times, but mum was expert at soothing him and they've always been affectionate, so I've got used to them kissing and cuddling in front of me. Mum always asked about school and I'd tell her lies about what I'd learnt which kept her happy. Dad would always show me his models: he called himself an artist, although he'd never displayed his work and refused to lower himself by joining the commercialised art-world, as it's so full of 'rich bastards who wouldn't understand art if it was crammed up their arseholes'. Dad always made me laugh and we did a lot together. We liked movies and he'd let me stay up into the small hours, even on school nights, watching his favourite films. I've got lots of happy memories of times with Dad.

Dad made my favourite toy: a doll – a strange-looking creature that had no name, but that I had always loved and kept in my bed. It might seem a bit strange for a boy to have a doll, but it was just a toy creature – anyway I loved him the best. Dad was really generous in his art and he'd always be making me things and working out what I'd like next. He was thoughtful like that.

Sometimes I'd get a bit bored and wish I had a brother or sister, or that I could go out more with Robbo, but Mum and Dad were good company and I understood that I was needed to help them out with things around the house. Honestly I didn't mind. It sounds weird, but I did all the cleaning, cooking and washing, not because they made me, but I knew that they were busy and I had the time to do these things. I was proud to be able to help my parents in this way. I never complained.

Then one day Dad told me he and Mum were going away for a few days, which they had already done a number of times. I'm not scared of being alone; in fact, I'm pretty used to it now and enjoy my own company because I'm used to fending for myself and I'm the most domesticated individual in the house anyway. Looking after Trooper was a bit annoying as he could be quite aggressive and I hated taking him for walks as he would always attack any other dog we met, and even once bit a man who kicked him. Dad was furious and even though the man's leg was bleeding, he said he would sue the man for kicking his dog. Nothing ever came of it.

With my parents out of the way, I decided to do something I'd never done before. I went home with Robbo after school. I'd never actually been to a friend's house before. Mum and Dad don't really have any friends as they say each other is enough for them, which is quite sweet when you think about it. They don't go out much either, except for work purposes or when they disappear, as they do, for a few nights. So I went home with Robbo and was amazed to see how clean and tidy his house was. There were carpets that looked brand new and he had comfortable chairs and a sofa. It was the first time I had sat on a sofa and I marvelled at the way it curved to your back and felt so soft, softer than my lumpy mattress that was so damp and full of bedbugs. The walls had coloured paper over their smooth, flat surfaces and held shelves full of books or had paintings framed and tacked to the wall. It was all so new and exciting to my eyes, that people could live like this.

The whole house was so strange and fantastic, but I think I managed to keep my amazement hidden as I had practiced so often before. I could conceal the deepest emotions and was proud of my great skill of deception. Perhaps one day I could be an actor. What struck me most about the house was its overly hygienic cleanliness. His father was polite and shook my hand and his mother, after kissing him, asked me if I wanted to stay for tea. I nodded my head and smiled politely.

Just as I was about to suggest to Robbo that we go out to the park for a bit, his father came in and told him to settle down to his homework, to which Robbo dutifully agreed and told me to do the same. This wasn't my idea of fun – I never did my homework, certainly not at home. When it was tea-time I followed Robbo into the bathroom, wandering what he was doing and copied him when he washed his hands, wondering at this odd ritual. What was even weirder was that we all sat down together at a table and had to say a prayer before eating, even though Robbo had never shown any previous signs of being religious.

And then there was the food. It looked colourful; it seemed to be meat, vegetables and gravy – even though I desperately wanted fish and chips. The meat was okay, but a bit chewy and I managed to swallow a few of the vegetables without gagging. Bloody vegetables – I can't stand them and we never eat them anyway – I understand why now. Then we had an apple pie that scorched the inside of my mouth it was so hot and by the end of the meal I thanked Robbo's parents in my politest voice, willing my friend to release me from this god-awful situation. Their idea of fun was to sit round a table together and discuss topics that are frankly very dull and pointless. How glad I was that Mum and Dad didn't torture me this way. Robbo also had a younger brother who made rude remarks and I kept thinking that if he was my brother, then my Dad would have given him a good hiding by now and taught him to keep his mouth shut. I probably would punch him in the face if he talked to me like that.

The rest of the evening didn't go too well either, as I was amazed to find out that my friend wasn't even allowed to watch films with a 15 certificate, let alone the sort my Dad let me watch. When Robbo was ordered to bed at nine and told to say goodbye to me, I left with a feeling of relief that my own home life wasn't like this. In fact, it surprised me Robbo was as normal as he was with such tyrannical parents – although I was shocked when he told me his father had never so much as hit him. The colours of the house stayed in my head for a while: the curtains, wallpaper, flowers in vases, the food and Robbo's games and toys, as I strolled home via the off-licence.

I made the stupid mistake of telling Mum I'd been round to Robbo's house, hoping to make her laugh with my description of his weird house. I didn't know she'd tell Dad and he went mental. It was no use trying to explain to him. He clipped me round the ear a few times and that was painful and even when I tried to defend myself like he'd shown me to he still thumped his fist viciously right into my solar plexus, winding me and making me keel over into a foetus shape. Still not sure if he was angry or if this was just one of our play-fights, he grabbed my wrists and lifted me bodily by one hand so that I hung helplessly in front of him and he punched me again in the stomach. I'll admit that I blacked out and came round in the kitchen, to the sight of my Mum ticking me off and telling me that I should do what's good for me. It was a fair point and I eventually got up off the floor, which I realised now was very dirty, and made Dad a cup of tea. I told you, didn't I? Don't mess with my Dad. In any fight situation my Dad's the champ – you've got to hand it to him. He's in his forties now and I'm not exactly small. I'm really proud of him.

I didn't expect it then, but Dad grabbed my hair and I have to admit I flinched – call me a coward, yeah, yeah – but he didn't continue the fight. Instead he told me to bring Robbo round. At first I argued but he had a very determined look in his eyes, so I kept quiet, like I've learnt to. I'd never brought anyone round before in my life, but it was a reasonable request and Mum even got out the hoover, wanting to make a good impression.

So after an extremely dull day at school I walked up our street with a friend by my side to our semi-detached house, number 27, and even before I opened the door I could hear Trooper barking gruffly and growling. You need three keys to get into our house as Dad's really tight on security, and I let Robbo go in first and he stood there astounded so I had to give him a push to get him in and close the door. I heard him muttering something about the dirt and the stains on the walls, where there were walls, as most of them had either caved in or had holes where things were kept in storage. I could see his eyes become horrified but fascinated by the dead rats in the corner of the hall and the cockroaches that freely scuttled about on the damaged floorboards. I wrestled with Trooper, eventually shutting him in the cupboard under the stairs, where he whined pathetically.

We had no furniture of any note but the floors were littered with newspaper, burger cartons and general detritus now stuck and moulded over the years. It was my home and I was proud of it. I took him to the back room, which had boarded up windows and a naked bulb that made the room glow with a sickly orange mood. My Dad was in there watching a porn film. Robbo was shaking and too timid to speak as I roughly shoved him into the room. My Dad told him to sit on an upturned bucket, which he did with his eyes wide – exactly like Trooper always looks just before my Dad smacks him.

Dad's an imposing figure if you haven't met him. He's not that tall, but he's very wide and stocky, with iron-grey hair and little John Lennon glasses. Wearing only a crumpled t-shirt and boxers, he smiled at me, winked and told me to make a cup of tea. I'm still not sure what happened as I was out making the tea but when I returned with the drinks made, the two were laughing together. I let out Trooper who continued growling and scratching at me, only shutting up when I gave him some of his smelly biscuits, which he wolfed down as he probably hadn't been fed that day.

I beckoned to Robbo, who had to tear himself away from the film that graphically portrayed whatever fetish Dad was into then, and we went upstairs. By now, Robbo was staring wide-eyed and sweating nervously; making comments about wanting to go home, but I called him a chicken and he went sulkily quiet, but at least he stopped whinging. He looked slightly relieved when we got to my room because it was neater than the rest of the house and I had a television and stereo. He wasn't sure about the mattress in the corner and couldn't believe it was my bed. When he asked me where my duvet was I sniggered scornfully and felt a little sorry for him.

The sound of voices outside my room disturbed us and I looked up to see my Mum come out of her own room with a customer. She just wore a thin negligee and popped her head round the corner to say hi. Robbo's eyes narrowed with confusion, but I felt no need to explain. He was looking at her nipples, I could tell.

Instead I showed him my pride and joy: my toy made for me by Dad. Robbo took it in his hands and turned it over, his face becoming more perplexed like he could almost recognise something. The doll was an obscure figure; its limbs were misshapen and vaguely familiar. My friend took a strand of the doll's hair between his fingers and looked up at me.

"Human hair," I told him casually. His face contorted into a look of disapproval, so I told him the rest. "The body's made up of bones, fingers mainly. It's very clever isn't it? The way it almost looks normal. Dad made it."

"Fucking weird," he whispered. "Your family is fucking weird." He got up very decisively and said with a whimper, "I'm going home now."

That was when I started to feel a bit regretful, because he had always been such a good friend to me, but, after all, as Dad always says, "People never stay friends forever." Good things must always come to an end. The punch I took at him cracked his jawbone. Clutching it pathetically, Robbo got up and scampered downstairs.

Of course he couldn't open our specially adapted front door and once Dad had bound his mouth with gaffer tape he had become a limp victim and plaything for my parents. Dad didn't make me watch this time, for which I was grateful, so I turned on *The Weakest Link* instead and dialled for a pizza.

The rest was so much easier than you can imagine. I just had to tell the police that the two of us were walking alone when a gang attacked us and Dad even went to the trouble of beating me up a little to provide extra evidence with my new bruises to show me as a fellow victim. Nobody saw Robbo come into our house either – who would? Who the hell knows what their neighbours are up to?

The body parts were discovered ten miles away in a ditch and it made me laugh when I heard that the police are still searching for a violent gang of youths – I told you Dad's bloody clever at this sort of thing. No-one's going to catch my old man. He's the best.

Jeff Gardiner's collection of short stories, A Glimpse of the Numinous, *was published by Eibonvale Press. His contemporary novel,* Myopia, *explores bullying and prejudice – recently published by Crooked Cat Books. Both are available as paperbacks and e-books. Many of his short stories have appeared in anthologies, journals and webzines. He also has a work of non-fiction to his name. For more information please see his website at jeffgardiner.com and his blog jeffgardiner.wordpress.com.*

THE ALGORITHM
by Cameron Suey

Sometime during the third consecutive night spent huddled over the toilet, insides heaving and shuddering as I vomit forth what seems to be everything I've ever eaten, I realize what's happening. He's trying to poison me. It's all so elegant, so perfect and so clear that I start to laugh, but another barrage of retching forces me into silence.

The next morning, I throw the contents of my meager kitchen away, wrapping it three times in black plastic and burying it deep in the apartment's communal dumpster, to prevent some unfortunate transient from the crossfire of His wrath. I am out the door of the complex and halfway to the corner store when I realize: He knows, must know, where I would shop.

So instead, I pick a direction and walk, enjoying the chill winter air as it soothes the ragged shreds of my insides. I turn at random intervals, following an improbable path out of my neighborhood until I find a small grocery with an unfamiliar name. Once inside, I fill a small plastic shopping basket with foods and brands that once I would have never eaten. Soy milk. Tofu. Strange tins of ethnic foods whose ingredients I can't recognize. I can feel my stomach reborn in the anticipation of an untainted meal.

I prepare the food in a fog of nervous anticipation, trying to focus on savoring the exotic aromas and the grease-spitting sounds of the frying pan. When it is done, and the meal sits before me on the chipped and stained plate, I can only stare, paralyzed by doubt. By the time I can raise a single spoonful to my chapped and split lips, it has long ago grown cold.

It tastes clean, but this brings me no joy. So has every meal before this. An hour later, I try to tell myself that the mounting pain is only fear and anxiety. But before the stroke of midnight, I am again crouched in the dingy bathroom, surrendering the day's work into the porcelain mouth of the sewer.

I pack up the remaining food and dispose of it with the same care. I eat out the next day, layering debt onto the last of my credit cards in restaurants on the opposite side of town. I feel the eyes of every patron on me, and wonder if any of them are in His employ. By dark, it is clear that He is cleverer than I ever imagined. I am awash in despair as I spend another sleepless night gagging and sobbing on the tile floor. I imagine the Algorithm, the perfect predictive models at His disposal, charting my every move across the city with unerring accuracy. Every time I think I've outwitted Him, I walk willingly into His web.

There is nothing left to do but wait for the jaws of His trap to close, so I wander the city, a broken man. In a fit of misplaced hope, I buy a candy bar from a vending machine in a theater lobby, and hold it close, like a talisman. When I get home, I fill the bath a few inches deep with rust colored water, and hold the little plastic wrapped bundle beneath the water and squeeze. I know that I will see it, but it still breaks my heart. A thin, almost invisible stream of bubbles picks out the point where a foreign object has pierced the protective layer. Through the haze of gnawing hunger, I convince myself to try just one bite and to take my chances. This is a gamble that I do not win.

In the small hours of the morning, I press my fists into my empty protesting belly, and I imagine the legion of His followers. Sliding silently through the restaurants and produce aisles of my life, slipping hypodermic needles into carefully selected packages of food. They ruin and corrupt at His whim, surgical and efficient, before vanishing into the throng of the city at my approach. They have none of the compassion and love that I have. They are less than human.

With His fearful intellect pulling their strings, they will always be one step ahead of me, until I learn to think in new ways, to chart new cognitive pathways, and turn the game back upon Him. So, I tell myself, this is what I must do.

I spend the first day of my new life in the cramped living room of my apartment, organizing my thoughts with clean, sterile efficiency, and conserving what energy I can from my wasting body. Night brings the retching sickness, but all that arises is water and pills, half-digested in the bilious fluids.

The pills. Of course. Not for the first time, I feel a sharp twinge of respect for the crystalline perfection of His plans. I dump the last of my dozen prescriptions into the toilet and watch as they dissolve into pink and blue clouds.

On the third day, I am rocked with a sudden clarity and a sense of purpose that shocks me in its intensity. My will penetrates through the starvation malaise. I must win, or I will die. The rashes and sores inside my cheeks are deeper, and I can feel the gentle sway of loose teeth when I clench my jaw. He is still winning, but not for long. There is still time.

Water I can collect from the roof in a small army of cheap hardware store buckets. I know that somewhere in the byzantine plumbing of the aged building, there must be one of His infernally clever devices, a tiny pump, squatting like a predator and pulsing its vile contents into the water main. I'll have to give up bathing. A small sacrifice. The rain water will keep me alive for a while longer, but I must find a way to eat.

The answer comes to me in mismatched puzzle pieces over the next few days. While gently working another loose molar from my bleeding gums, the pieces suddenly snap together, and a warm smothering blanket of epiphany coats my aching frame. The clattering of the tooth into the sink basin is like the ringing of bells.

Late in the frigid afternoon, I begin another unconscious journey, drifting through the city on shaking and atrophied legs, knowing full well that He is watching. But this, my beautiful solution, is beyond even His reach.

I choose the house at random, and then, in one final attempt to baffle the Algorithm, turn around and choose another house across the narrow, tree-lined street. I sift through the mail. It's a small sample size, but enough to confirm the most necessary of facts. A single occupant.

The poor man is surprised to have a visitor at all, and his face contorts with fear as I force my way inside. I am flooded with guilt and regret as I push him to the floor and strike his skull with the crowbar I pull from the folds of my jacket.

No. I must steel myself. This is His fault. He has dragged us both to this moment, and this poor man, like me, is just another of His victims.

I make quick work of the meat, the muscle memories of summers spent hunting in the mountains flaring up with each quick cut, severing ligament from bone. I allow myself a quick bite, a feast to my shrunken and withered stomach. The iron and mineral salt taste floods my head like a vapor and I bawl like a child in relief.

I waste nothing, and leave behind only slick bones and offal. I want so much to thank this man for his sacrifice, but I can think of no fitting tribute, so I whisper my gratitude to his remains. When I have the meat wrapped in plastic and packed tight into my rucksack, I light a single candle on the top floor of the little house, and turn the gas stove on high.

I'm not yet home when I hear the low rumble of the explosion, a wave of thunder from the distance that crashes over me. The pulsing lights of fire engines highlight the black column of smoke rising into the sky. I walk on, leaving the chaos behind.

For the first time in more than a month, I sleep like a babe, my body healing as pure and untainted nutrients penetrate my cells. I am not yet well, but after a few more meals, I will be ready, once more, to fight Him. I know I can beat Him now. I know the Algorithm can only predict the actions of my past self, bound by the laws and morals of the old world.

That world is dead.

I am a free man.

Cameron Suey is a California native living in San Francisco with his wife (who can occasionally be convinced to edit his work, as long as it's not too gross) and infant daughter. He works as a writer and producer in the games industry, and along with several other talented writers, won the WGA Award for Videogame Writing in 2009 for Star Wars: The Force Unleashed. *He can be found on the web at http://thejosefkstories. com, where he writes about writing, horror, and other influences, and on twitter as @josefkstories where he promises not to bore you with tales of what he had for breakfast.*

AGAINST THE BACK WALL

by Dan Howarth

Neil tried phoning her one more time before he left but, as with the other five calls he had made that day, he was sent through to voicemail. He had already left a message and decided against leaving another. Despite feeling paranoid about the situation he was determined not to let his paranoia transmit itself to Sally. The last thing he wanted to do was scare her off at this point.

Glancing at the clock in the kitchen Neil began to hurry around, collecting his water bottle and sweatbands from the cluttered breakfast bar before grabbing his squash racket and heading through the front door. It was only when he locked it that he realised he had forgotten his phone. Uttering a vicious *fuck* under his breath he charged back into the kitchen to retrieve it.

Thankfully he only lived a two minute walk from the leisure centre where he was due to play and he used the short walk to try to focus his mind on the game ahead. The summer sun hung lazily over the artificial football pitch where a few sweaty youths were kicking a ragged-looking football around. One of them shouted over as he walked past.

"Oi! Can you get that other ball?"

Despite his initial annoyance at the way the young man addressed him, Neil jogged over to the nearby ball and attempted to kick it back over the fence, wincing as the ball clattered into it. He picked the ball up and threw it over with a smile.

"That's why I play squash mate."

The youth that had spoken to him was stockily built. He showed signs of a hard life – menial labour and binge drinking were etched into the premature lines on his face. He didn't laugh or smile or even change his expression, he simply collected the spare ball and punted it to one of his friends before jogging back to the rest of the group. Neil felt a chill despite the summer heat; looking back over his shoulder at the group he was glad that it hadn't been dark when he had encountered them.

As he reached the door to the court he received a text message and rushed to fish his phone out of his pocket. To his disappointment it was from Lee.

They've changed the code for the door again – 1280Z. We're on court 3.

Neil sighed. He hadn't heard from Sally all day; this was the longest he had gone without speaking to her for months. Since before Tracy left him now he thought about it. He keyed in the code and let himself into the squash courts. The corridor was dark and painfully hot; the radiators were always on in here regardless of the time of year. On the left hand side of the wall were the doors to the three courts, the door to court 3 left ajar at the far end of the corridor awaiting his entrance. The right hand side of the corridor was taken up by a staircase to the balcony above from where spectators could watch matches or players could linger waiting for their forty minutes on court.

Neil wasn't quite sure how he had come to play squash in the first place. He had always been almost exclusively interested in football whereas Lee enjoyed a wide range of sports. Lee had asked him to fill in as his opponent one night and the routine had sprung from there. What had begun as a friendly game had blossomed into a competitive series of games with both players running themselves to near-exhaustion trying to better the other. The game had taken on more meaning for Lee and Neil over the years. They were both pigeonholed into jobs that never blossomed into careers, shared a friendship group that had dwindled to nothing, their lives reduced to a collection of possessions and numbers on bank statements. Their weekly game of squash gave them back some of the fire of their youth. When they felt the competitive adrenaline in their veins the years slipped away and for forty minutes a week they were driven and hungry once again. Neil smiled to himself at the thought of winning again this week, his male pride suddenly reinvigorated at the thought.

The court had seen better days. As usual it took Neil a few seconds of fumbling to get the door shut – it never quite seemed to fit into the frame. The walls surrounding the court bore the scars of hundreds of matches, thousands of coloured scrapes exhibiting where rackets had recovered balls from the corner, the white emulsion stained a dirty yellow where sweat had never been cleaned off. The courts had been built in the eighties and Neil was willing to bet that the floors hadn't been swept since: the layer of dirt was palpable, the wooden boards pockmarked with stains of spilled blood and energy drinks. Lee stood in the centre of the court wearing his green tracksuit jacket over the top of his white squash kit.

"I've only just arrived mate, don't worry." He said as he unzipped his jacket and placed it carefully in the corner of the court.

They both took their rackets out of their sports bags and took a position almost side by side to warm up the ball. The squash ball had to be warmed up so it bounced properly; the two used this as their opportunity to warm themselves up, stretching away the tensions of the working week from their muscles. As was their routine they used this opportunity to catch up before the serious business of the competitive game began.

"How has work been this week? Any closer to becoming Lee Worrall – senior sales analyst?"

Thwack went the ball as they smacked it off the back wall to each other.

"Nah. Another twenty-something woman promoted ahead of me. No doubt in the name of diversity." *Thwack.*

"I know how you feel. Sometimes I just wonder if I should quit and start over. Maybe now is the time, you know, not having any dependents and all." *Thwack.*

"Maybe it's an idea mate. You've got to consider the future soon before it's too late." *Thwack.*

"Spot on mate. Anything new with you… How's Sally?" Neil glanced over at Lee as he said this, sneaking a look at his friend in the corners of his peripheral vision.

THWACK. "She's OK mate. Thanks for asking."

Lee picked up the ball as Neil hit it back to him again.

"I think this is ready mate. Shall we start?"

Neil won the toss and served first. He immediately took a big lead in the first game and surprised himself by how well he was playing. Normally he won a lot of points by hitting the ball hard into the far corners of the court where he knew that Lee, who carried a few extra pounds, would be unable to get to it in time. Yet today he felt light on his feet and energised. He played some surprisingly deft shots that seemed to catch Lee on his heels and he was unable to move quickly enough to return them.

As he came to serve for final point of the game, Neil looked over at Lee. His face was flush, his bald, slightly bloated head was already slick with sweat and he lifted up his t-shirt to mop the moisture away from his eyes. Neil caught sight of his friend's belly as he lifted his shirt, and found himself vaguely repulsed by the flabby white gut he saw. Lee had really let himself slide over the last few months. His diet had regressed to almost exclusively processed food and unlike Neil this forty minute session of squash was his only exercise for the week.

Neil served out the match and easily claimed the next two games, yet didn't feel the rush of victory that he normally did. Lee, whilst his swearing and complaining about marginal decisions were still there, didn't seem to have his heart in the game. He was still sweating profusely but was nowhere near mobile enough to keep up with Neil and his lack of foot speed had helped to grind down his patience to nothing.

After four quick games Neil was unsurprised to hear Lee asking for a drinks break. He found himself slightly irritated by this. It wasn't often he was able to comfortably beat Lee like this and he wanted to make the most of the opportunity that had presented itself. He drank from his bottle of Lucozade and leaned his back on the plastered wall, feeling it cool his skin through the moist patches on his t-shirt. Lee was stood opposite him, and despite sweating profusely he hadn't yet cracked open either of the bottles of water he had brought with him. He was stood, head bent, typing furiously into his Blackberry and muttering incomprehensibly under his breath.

"You alright mate?" Neil said, frowning at his friend's behaviour.

Lee looked up as if startled to see Neil still stood there.

"Yeah, yeah. Just trying to sort a few things out for work still, some people are just bloody useless. Can they just listen to a simple instruction?"

Neil muttered some sort of vague agreement to the question. He had rarely seen Lee so worked up. He made a mental note to bring work up more often when they played in future; it was clearly having a hugely detrimental effect on his friend's performance. Lee's phone buzzed again and he checked his message quickly, snatching his phone up from his kit bag. He paused momentarily and then laughed savagely before dropping the phone haphazardly into the bag with a happy "Done!"

Lee jogged over into his position on the far side of the court ready to receive Neil's serve. He crouched low and focussed his gaze on his friend as he waited. Lee grinned at Neil but there was no friendliness or recognition in his face. His smile was a deterrent, a warning of what was to come. He met Neil's eye – "Game on, mate!"

The game was a stark contrast to the previous ones: Lee played some fantastic shots, out-hustling and out-thinking Neil with ease. He quickly seized the initiative from Neil and won the game comfortably. Afterwards, he wiped the sweat from his forehead and asked Neil disparagingly if he was "Ready to go again?"

The next game was intense. Neil rose to the challenge set down by his reinvigorated friend and began to work hard, feeling the sweat coat his limbs as he charged around the small court. Both men grunted and swore as luck and skill turned their backs on them, the urgent fall of their footsteps on the wooden floor punctuated only by the dull thud of the small rubber ball being hit hard against plaster. As the score moved beyond the necessary nine points for victory, aggression began to bubble very close to the surface for both men.

They continued their tense, perfectly choreographed game of squash, each man stepping forward to place the ball in an impossible spot for the other, only to see his best efforts rebuffed with a pant of exertion and the return shot placing him in a similarly tricky situation. This was until Neil played a hard straight shot away from Lee into far corner of the court. He half-turned to see where his rival was but was clattered so hard from behind that he was barely able to put his arms up in time to stop his face smashing into the wall.

Prising himself away from the wall, more dazed by the shock of being shoulder barged than in actual pain, Neil turned to Lee who was stood behind him, panting with exertion. He was about to speak when Lee cut him off.

"What the fuck do you think you are doing?"

"Excuse me? You just rammed me into the fucking wall you prick!"

"Only because you didn't move, you deliberately stopped me from returning that ball."

"Did I fuck." Neil felt anger rising in his voice, the volume escalating along with his temper.

"You saw me coming and stepped across. That should be my point and put me one point away from winning."

"Not a chance – I'll replay it, *at best*, but nothing else. You're a fucking cheat mate."

"Fine." There was an air of finality in Lee's voice, Neil knew from his tone – the tone he normally adopted when things didn't go his way, that things were definitely not fine.

Neil turned away as Lee walked over to get the ball and tried to calm himself before making a concerted effort to win the next point.

He felt the pain before he even heard any movement behind him. With a dull thud the small rubber ball hit him square in the middle of the back. Neil jumped forward in agony. This time he was genuinely hurt and felt tears welling up in his eyes that were much more than shock. He skipped slightly as he gingerly took a few steps before dropping his racket and rubbing the spot where the ball had hit him, it was already sporting a swollen, red welt.

"What the fuck do you think you are doing?" Neil forgot any pretence that Lee was his friend and let the hurt he felt show in his voice.

Lee dropped his racket as soon as Neil finished his sentence. He lumbered towards his friend, Neil becoming acutely aware of just how big his friend was as he watched him advance with his hands balled into meaty fists.

"I'll tell you what I'm fucking doing *mate*, I'm getting even with you starting right now." Without warning he punched Neil hard in the stomach, knocking the breath from his lungs and bringing more tears to his eyes. Neil doubled over and spat onto the grubby wooden floor, panting and gasping.

"I'm no mug Neil, I know that you've been sleeping with Sally." The anger that had been in Lee's voice before he hit Neil had now given way to a calculated calm. Neil got the impression that this incident had been planned a long time before it actually happened.

Sweat poured from his forehead but not the hot, bestial sweat that came with exercise but the cold, reluctant sweat of fear.

"That punch felt so so good Neil. You've no idea how long I wanted to do that for, in fact it's been since I saw you two together just before Christmas. This has been festering for quite some time – hasn't it chum?"

Neil was momentarily speechless. He had first slept with Sally just before Christmas, possibly the night Lee was talking about.

"But if you have known for that long why not confront me – or her – long before this?"

Lee smiled at him, the grin a replica of the cold, formidable one he had used before the match started.

"Well because these things take planning *mate*, to get the maximum effect sometimes you have to put the work in, plan it. People that act out of instinct, without thinking, tend to get hurt. Like you for example." Lee laughed harshly and unnecessarily. It was only as the hollow sound reverberated around the court they had used and the one next to it that Neil realised that the building was silent. There were no people using the other courts. He cocked his head, desperate to hear the sound of someone else, another person that could help him. There was none.

Lee noticed what Neil was doing and fixed him with a mocking look.

"I've booked all three courts for the next four hours *mate*, you are mine until they come to lock up."

At the confirmation of his fate, Neil surged up from his crouching position and hurled himself at his friend. Lee saw him coming and with deceptive speed for a man his size neatly stepped out of the way before connecting his fist hard with the side of Neil's nose. Blood exploded outwards, falling as bright red droplets hitting the floor and turning a shade of dirty brown.

"Don't waste your energy trying to run and don't waste your breath trying to apologise. You're in here with me for a long time and believe me I will make you pay for what you have done to me. You've taken the love of my life away from me. You turned her into someone I could barely look at. Do you know how that feels?!"

"Yes!" Neil cried, his face covered in fresh blood and his voice sounding like he had a heavy cold. "I do know – Tracey fucked off and left me remember? And your wife was the only person who was there for me. She ran to me and although it was wrong, I took it because I had nothing else left. I'm truly sorry."

"You're truly sorry? I've heard that elsewhere actually. From someone else today, in fact it was one of the last things she said to me before they went to work on her."

Neil felt as if a cold, dirty hand had begun to squeeze his insides.

"Before *who* went to work on her Lee?"

Lee looked at his friend, the lower half of Neil's face covered in blood that was beginning to dry onto his skin in dark, dirty flakes whilst the rest of his face seemed to be losing colour by the second.

"I couldn't bring myself to harm her – twelve years of marriage and I barely raised my voice to her. But she needed to be taught a lesson. So I hired some help. It's funny really, if you make enquiries with the right people, it isn't particularly difficult to dig down through the levels of humanity and find some real nasty fuckers that will do pretty much anything you ask if the price is right. It took two nights drinking in *The Stag's Heart,* which we both know is a complete shithole, and before I know it I have some bloke's number who is willing to do you both for five grand. Can't argue with that."

Neil began to sob quietly to himself as Lee spoke down to him. The salty tears mixed with the metallic taste of blood on his teeth. His shoulders heaved as he tried to suppress the sound of his crying, his arms hanging in front of him limp and useless. Neil lifted his head from his chest as he heard the front door to the squash courts open and bang against the outside wall. He screamed for help at the top of his voice, the sound thickened by the amount of swallowed blood that coated his throat. Lee simply laughed and looked at the clock with a simple smile and a hollow chuckle.

"Oh good. They're bang on time."

The sound of many pairs of feet ascended the stairs and five figures stepped into view on the balcony above the court. The smallest of the five, a small, overweight bald man wearing a black leather jacket and several earrings, leant with his arms over the balcony. His meaty hands were clasped together and his sleeves had ridden up to reveal a network of tattoos snaking up his arms. The other four, taller figures stood behind him. Hands behind their backs, they wore bright hooded tops with the hoods pulled up to obscure their faces. Neil guessed that whilst they would be doing the dirty work tonight, the bald man would end up with most of the fee.

"Is this who you paid us five grand to do? Your bird and this little piss ant? We wanted a challenge."

The man laughed falsely. The figures behind him didn't move or say anything. Their inactivity unnerved Neil; there was clearly going to something heinous committed here tonight yet the men on the balcony didn't seem in the least bit bothered. Neil squinted, and thought he could make out some features in the shadows but couldn't be sure.

"Looks like you've started the party early Mr Best, I hope you aren't thinking of asking for your money back just because you've had a few digs yourself."

"I wouldn't dream of it. I paid the money for the service and I know it will be performed satisfactorily." Lee's voice was full of fake bravado. Neil could tell by his body language that he was already intimidated.

"Good good. So are you still on for, you know, finishing this lad off? We'll do the groundwork and you do the cutting as discussed?"

Neil gasped as the bald man produced a machete as long as his forearm from inside the leather jacket. "Lee you can't be fucking serious mate. You did this to Sally? Oh my God. What the fuck has *happened* to you?"

The bald man leered down at the miserable pair inside the court. Neil had once again sunk to his haunches whilst Lee stood over him, his sweat turning cold on his t-shirt raising the hairs on his arms.

"But he couldn't do his missus in, could you, Mr Office Job? He was all high and mighty in the pub when he'd had a few beers, bossing us around, but when we showed up at his house earlier he got nervous – didn't you flower?" This time the bald man laughed properly, a fierce, unpleasant sound. Lee looked away from the balcony and down at his feet as the bald man continued to talk. "He pissed off to work and left us to it. We had a lot of fun once you had left son." The bald man smiled, lines appearing around his eyes and mouth that didn't make him look any happier, simply more menacing. "So here it is, your last chance. Are you gonna do him or shall we take over and finish this pathetic little job for you?"

Lee looked at Neil, who was almost cowering in the far corner of court. His eyes met those of his friend and despite the anger he felt looking at that face, he could not bring himself to answer yes.

"Just do it for me," he shouted up to the balcony, "I paid you for this service and I want a good job doing. Do it quickly and do it well. And make sure you stick to your agreement. Don't go contacting me asking for money cos you've pissed it all up the wall. Sort this mess out and leave me alone. OK?"

The bald man's eyes lit up as Lee finished speaking, colour rising up through his neck and into his cheeks. The look in his eyes rapidly changed from bored indifference to something far more threatening, but then his face relaxed and once again he began to smile.

"Oh, you have made me so happy to hear you say that Mr Best. So happy! All the way here the boys were begging me to let them hurt you. You see, they think this is a boring job, something below their normal level of expertise. They want to have a little fun, enjoy their work. You know how it is."

Neil made for the door, pushing past Lee on his way to seize the handle that was concealed inside a rut in the door. He yanked it with all his strength, screaming in frustration as he failed to move it. He punched the door hard, leaving a dirty, bloody handprint on it. He began to cry as the bald man continued to talk.

"The thing is, you are a very obvious type of person Mr Best. You had a vague idea of something you wanted doing and immediately looked for someone you classed as 'beneath you' to do it. You viewed this as menial work and us as some sort of manual labour. Well to be honest, I don't really care much for your lack of manners and since you paid me up front, as your type always do, I guess I have no reason to keep you around. At the end of the day you are just one more witness…"

Lee began to holler and shout as the bald man stepped backwards from the balcony's ledge with a small sarcastic wave. As if on cue, the four men behind him stepped forward and stood on the ledge above the court, their faces level with the high lighting, close to the roof, towering over the two men below. They pulled their hoods back and Neil found himself looking at the youths he had encountered on the AstroTurf. Yet their faces were different; he made eye contact with the lead youth and saw that he looked younger, more alive than he had done before. He eyed Neil with amusement – there was no blank gaze or look of indifference now, the youth had a look of determination in his eyes. He now looked as if he had a purpose.

As one they dropped from the balcony to the court, landing with a dull thud on the dusty wooden boards below. The lead youth eyed the two men in front of him, alive to the task ahead. He smiled and it sent electricity down Neil's spine. It was the smile of a predator, a killer, a deviant. "I'm going to enjoy this," was all he said.

The white walls soon became a gallery of red.

Dan Howarth *is a horror writer based in the North West of England. No Monsters Allowed is the first of what he hopes to be many credits in 2013. Dan's influences include Stephen King, Gary McMahon and Adam Nevill. He is currently working on a novella which he hopes will be completed early 2013. When he isn't writing horror Dan can usually be found on the football pitch or shouting from the terraces.*

KILLER CON
by A.D. Barker

Bundy continues, the audience in the palm of his hand, "… So the second time I escaped, I hid down in Tallahassee under the name Chris Hagen, bummed around for a few weeks, then one night I broke into a sorority house at Florida State and well… I guess I raped and murdered two more young women."

The crowd bursts into applause. Ted Bundy, stood on the stage with microphone in hand, looks a little taken aback by the overwhelming response. He dares a slight smile. He is clearly a handsome man; many of the figures in the audience are women, most look adoringly up at him. The applause tapers out.

"After that…. It's hard for me to remember all the details," he says. "Memories are untrustworthy, unreliable. When you're possessed by such wickedness as I was, you forget things, it all gets pretty hazy."

A voice shouts out from the back of the room, "How did you kill 'em?" It was a man's voice, but Bundy struggles to pinpoint where the voice came from in the glaring spotlight.

"I…" He falters, lingering over the ghastly details, wondering how best to explain what he did to those girls while they lay sleeping in their beds. He coughs, clearing his throat. "I bludgeoned and strangled them." The crowd rips into applause once again, wolf-whistling and yelling their respect and awe for Bundy. "I attacked several girls that night," he continues. "But I found out later that only two of the girls died, the others survived." Then, as an afterthought, adds, "I murdered the first two… the ones I took my time over."

The whoops and hollers continue, the crowd clearly enraptured by Bundy's every word.

"I moved onto Lake City where I abducted a twelve year old girl who I bit at and fucked like an animal, finally dumping her body under a pig shed. Fitting I thought." This raises the biggest applause of this macabre seminar, the sound thundering around the hall at an almost deafening pitch. Finally it subsides, allowing Bundy to continue. He looks slightly uncomfortable, bewildered almost.

"I was caught again, for the final time, a couple of nights later by a Pensacola Patrol Officer while I was out driving a stolen V-Dub," said Bundy, followed by boos and hisses from the audience. "I resisted arrest, taking on the police Officer, hoping to God he would kill me."

The audience suddenly quietens, clearly unsure of what to make of this last statement. Bundy uses the silence to confess something remarkable. He closes his eyes, blocking out the shadowed audience, and the bright, intrusive spotlight, and speaks in a soft and low tone. "I wish he had killed me, I needed to be stopped. I had such evil within me. It haunted me every minute of every day…. still does," he adds, quietly. "I never figured out where it came from… never. It was like a cancerous poison that grew in me, twisting my very being. I was the guy next door, no one suspected me of anything. It took years for the cops to figure out my modus operandi. I guess normality was my greatest weapon."

Perhaps sensing that he was in danger of losing the audience with this raw honesty, Bundy then stepped up the talk again by giving his thoughts on the media circus that surrounded his trail. He answered questions from the audience and for the most part remained as witty, intelligent and as charming as his legend suggested he was. With a standing ovation, Bundy left the stage with a smile and a wave to his adoring fans.

After the Bundy seminar, most patrons filed back out into the main signing auditorium. Many queuing to get the signatures of, and have their pictures taken with, big name Guests such as Henry Lee Lucas and Jeffrey Dahmer. While most did make beelines straight for the "star attractions", as it were, there was still much interest in lesser known yet equally fascinating Guests such as Herman Webster Mudgett, who, under the alias Dr. Henry Howard Holmes, was one of America's first serial killers. H.H. Holmes had built and opened a hotel in Chicago for the World's Fair in 1893; a three-storey, block-long building which was later dubbed the "Murder Castle". Most of Holmes' victims were female, either employees of the hotel, or lovers or even hotel guests. Victims were locked in soundproofed bedrooms which had been fitted with gas lines allowing Holmes to asphyxiate them at will. Others were taken to the basement of the hotel where Holmes would meticulously dissect and strip bodies of flesh. As a "Doctor", Holmes had many contacts at local medical schools and would sell skeletons and organs without ever being questioned. He was eventually caught however and hanged in 1896, when he was just thirty-four years of age. He was a particularly fascinating gentleman to speak to.

By the mid-afternoon the convention was in full swing. You can spend a lot of your time simply walking round and round the huge auditorium, as I did. There is just so much to see. At one point I passed several of the Guests having publicity shots taken together: a jovial looking Fred West having his picture taken with Myra Hindley, and almost randomly, the Japanese serial killer Tsutomu Miyazaki, who ate the hands of the four little girls he raped and murdered. They looked like they were having a good time. This was followed by a scowling, knife-wheedling Ottis Toole who stood with a smiling Charlie Starkweather (who does look a lot like James Dean!) followed in turn by a memorable photograph of a beaming Aileen Wuornos embracing a somber looking Belle Gunness.

There is much to see and do. Aside from the star signings, there are countless stalls selling t-shirts, figures, posters and other such memorabilia. You will need to bring plenty of money mind, as things do tend to be fairly expensive. Moreover, there are stalls selling hotdogs, burgers and the like. Plus, given the nature of the convention itself, there is even one eatery selling human flesh. This stall is costly though. But if you have the money (and if you have the patience to wait in the lengthy queues) then I highly recommend it. Very tasty!

I also discovered in one corner of the auditorium a

rather touching tribute to those killers who have yet to pass over. Pictures were displayed beneath the names, which were engraved on beautifully grafted plaques. There was Dennis Nilson, Richard Ramirez, David Berkowitz, Peter Sutcliffe and of course, Charles Manson.

Many fans had laid flowers.

Later in the day I stopped and spoke with John Wayne Gacy. He was dressed as Pogo the Clown and looked just splendid as he entertained passing folk with prat falls and balloon tricks. Gacy had this to say about the convention: "Well, it's my first time here at Killer Con, and at first I really didn't know what to expect. But the fans are crazy man, just crazy. If they ask me again, I'd be happy to come every goddamn year."

I asked him if there was anyone he himself was excited to meet and his answer was simple.

"Gein," he said, his clown's face smiling widely. "He's like the motherfuckin' godfather!"

I asked Gacy why Gein is so-well renowned when he was far from prolific. Gacy stood thinking for a moment, then said, "Hey man, it's not how many you've killed, it's about your style. Gein sure had style... shit he pulled man, Jesus H. Christ. I for one am damned excited."

And he wasn't the only one who was excited. Most had come to see Ed Gein, who was to make a special appearance during an evening seminar in the great hall. Gein hadn't been doing any signings during the day, nor any photographs; in fact, no one had even laid eyes on this legendary figure yet and excitement was getting high.

By evening the main event had arrived. The great hall filled within minutes, seemingly bursting with folk. Seating towards the front of the stage had been reserved for several of the Guests themselves. Gacy, now out of his clown make-up and costume, sat talking and laughing with Fritz Haarmann, murderer of twenty-seven boys and young men, and the Red Ripper, Andrei Chikatilo, who murdered considerably more, while Ted Bundy was seen talking to two young brunettes. Most though waited patiently and silently for the big moment to arrive.

As the audience settled down, the lights high in the rafters dimmed and a murmuring silence of anticipation felt over the hall. Low lights lit up the stage, revealing a set wonderfully and effectively dressed in grotesqueries. A chair sat in the centre of the stage fashioned from human bones, next to which stood a small table draped in skin, upon which lay a female skull and a glass of water. The backdrop was a mosaic of bones.

Nothing happened for a full five minutes, the audience shuffling with restlessness, then without warning a lone figure walked out onto the stage. It was a man no one seemed to recognise, only adding to the anticipation in the air. The man was smartly dressed in a pristine white suit and a large Stetson. He smiled and introduced himself to the audience:

"Good evening, Ladies and Gentlemen, and welcome to tonight's main attraction. My name is Bunny Gibbons. Please permit me to tell you a brief story – In 1958 I bought a beaten up 1949 Ford Sedan at an auction in Wisconsin." Gibbons paused dramatically, then added, "It was the car once owned by this evening's very special guest."

Clearly a showman, Mr. Gibbons allowed this piece of information to hang in the air for a moment, then continued, "During the 1950s I was a Funfair owner in Illinois. On learning about the auction I raced to Wisconsin and successfully outbid all. I paid $750, a princely sum in 1958 believe me. I first displayed the vehicle in Seymour, Wisconsin in July that same year, charging folk 25 cents to see and have their pictures taken next to the car. In the first two days my attraction pulled in more than two thousand visitors. If it wasn't for the authorities in Wisconsin I'd have been a millionaire!" The audience laughed along with the Funfair owner. Allowing a moment for the audience to settle, Bunny Gibbons slowly takes off his large Stetson and earnestly held it to his chest.

"The car was used by tonight's guest," he begins, "to transport the bodies he dug up from Plainfield Cemetery and took back to his dilapidated farmhouse. There he indulged in unspeakable acts of wickedness…" The crowd roars into a frenzy at this. Over the cheering of the audience, Bunny Gibbons shouts, "Ladies and gentleman, give a warm welcome to Edward Gein."

When the frail, little man shuffled out onto the stage, the audience went wild. Those who were sat then stood and cheered, whistling and clapping furiously. Ed Gein for his part gave a brief wave and then sat straight on his chair of bones.

Finally the standing ovation subsided, allowing Ed Gein to run his hand along the (literal) arm of the chair and say slyly, 'Ah, feels like I'm back at home.'

The audience went crazy for a further three minutes at that little wisecrack.

Once the room had finally settled Ed Gein took us through his life, first explaining that he was born in La Crosse, Wisconsin in 1906 to George and Augusta Gein. He spoke of his love and lifelong devotion to his mother. The audience were respectfully quiet and listened to every word, but I got the feeling most just wanted him to hurry and get to his years of grave-robbing, and ultimately, the murders he committed. He did touch on these subjects, explaining how he made belts out of women's nipples and wastepaper baskets from human flesh, but mostly Gein spoke about his childhood, of growing up in Wisconsin during the depression and of course, his mother.

He did however strongly hint that he murdered his own brother in 1944 and also spoke in great length about how he felt when his mother died of a stroke little over a year later, and how that ultimately led to his obsession of digging up and stealing bodies from the local cemetery. It was a fascinating talk, but I did feel that the majority of the audience were slightly disappointed he didn't go into more detail about his macabre activities.

That said, overall, most did feel that Killer Con ended on a high note and were already looking forward to next year's event. The convention's organisers explained that they believe the success of Killer Con comes from man's timeless fascination with murderers and all things macabre.

Jay Cawthorne, one of founders of Killer Con said, "There is part of us – all of us – that longs to kill, to take another life. It's just part of what makes us human, yet most of us have been conditioned, civilized. But still we all admire those few who, for whatever reason, have been born without compassion, without remorse – born with an inability to feel, to love. They become icons. They show what we could be without the shackles of morality."

Jay is hoping for a far bigger turnout next year as word begins to spread, and the profile of Killer Con is raised. I'll certainly be attending again, if only lured by the rumours of a very, very special guest…

The word is that next year's star attraction may very well be none other than the most famous serial killer in history, at last revealing his true identity:

Jack the Ripper.

A.D. Barker was born in Derby in 1975. He has had several short stories published in Morpheus Tales *magazine, and wrote and directed the 'lost' independent feature film,* A Reckoning. *He is currently working on his first novel.*

PIRANHA
by Steve Byrne

Vietnam 1967

LZ Betsy-Mae. What a dumb name for a military base. Its namesake had been the wife of the fat-gut CO who'd first commanded the place.

Lightning Boy spat into the red-brown dirt and looked around him, stowing the last of his shit into his pack.

Betsy-Mae was a clearing bombed into the jungle, encircled by razor wire and machine gun posts – a base of operations founded to launch incursions against the remote enemy. Satellite fire bases filled with heavy artillery protected Betsy-Mae from attack by guerrillas or NVA units, so that it could continue to be a jump off point for its own particular brand of search and destroy. The bases were little barbed spots of America dripped into the foreign landscape.

Within the perimeter, the LZ was a dirty collection of canvas, sandbags and bunkers, collected around a helicopter landing pad of compacted earth. The smell of wet canvas and burning shit from the latrines wafted in the air. Bare-chested marines humped sandbags or constructed new buildings, sat around cleaning their weapons or reading dog-eared copies of *Playboy*.

Lightning tuned out the sound of their banter as he hoisted his pack and followed the straggling line of the patrol out through the gate, leaving the lucky mofos behind. None of them looked his way. They continued hanging out washing, playing baseball and shooting the shit in huddled groups outside the bunkers. Somewhere a radio was playing Johnny Cash.

The brass never cut a brother any slack. He was fresh out of hospital and straight back into Indian Country, accompanied by a bunch of rednecks, lifers and FNGs. Some motherfucker somewhere wanted him dead.

Not that he was strictly alive in the first place. Oh yeah, the medics had patched him up just fine, told him how remarkably he'd recovered from the bullet wound. But he was changed. This wasn't life any more. Even before the temple incident, he'd been going through the motions, aiming his gun and keeping his shit tight, not allowing himself to think of anything but his DEROS – Date of Expected Return Overseas.

But after the temple, the change had set in deep. It had been bad shit back there, unbelievable shit. And when you see that the world ain't what you think it is, everything else you think you understand takes on a new meaning. What was there after DEROS? Back to Detroit, jiving on the street? Takin' shit every day because it was all that was fed to him? No way, man. No more.

All his life he'd been a runaway train, rollin' down a pre-determined track towards the end of his days. Then he'd seen the things inside the temple, been touched and now he understood. He'd seen the light, as his grandma would say. But it wasn't no light of God, and it wasn't no light of the Devil neither. Something had switched the points. But the train was a heavy mother, and the brakes weren't too good, and somewhere along the line he'd taken on passengers – and he sure as shit didn't want to see their faces.

He scanned the men in his patrol as they marched reluctantly across the rough dirt road and obliquely into the undergrowth.

Like most platoons they could be divided into two broad groups: the juicers and the heads. Alcoholics or dopeheads. Whichever it was, you had to take something to help you function in this country – or to make you forget your function. The juicers tended to be Republican-voting, hard-ass lifers – career soldiers, or good all-American boys fighting for God and country. People like Mason, the Beach Boy type who liked to push around the smaller guys. A school bully with an M-16. Or Ryan, the dark haired Radio Telephone Operator. Ryan had penetrating little eyes and a skulking gait. Creepy guy. But he was also a loud mouth, and everyone knew the rumours about him were true. He was a double veteran – a guy who'd screwed a gook woman then shot her. Mason, Ryan and a couple of other guys enjoyed shit like that.

Although he didn't do that much MJ, Lightning felt more at home with the heads. They were usually draftees, considered jerk-offs by the lifers. They were marking time here, getting high, listening to good music, trying to stay away from trouble. But you could depend on many of them when things got hot.

Ratman, his New York Italian fire team leader, was one such guy. He was the base's fixer, the guy who could get hold of anything, no matter what it took to get it.

But one thing Ratman couldn't do was avoid this patrol.

Lightning turned to see Ratman plodding along behind him. Rat surveyed Lightning wearily and raised his eyebrows in a gesture which said *same shit, different day.*

"Where the fuck are we goin', Rat?" asked Gull, the tall machine-gunner behind them. Gull was the only Texan Lightning knew who wasn't known as Tex. He was also the only Texan Lightning knew who wasn't a redneck Chuck son-of-a-bitch.

Ratman shrugged. "They don't tell me shit," he said without turning around.

"Another fucking fishing mission," came a grumbling voice from further down the line.

"Yeah, an' guess who gets to be the fucking maggot." This came from The Scholar, the fair-haired dude with glasses who walked in front of Lightning.

"Now don't you worry yourself none, boy," Gull drawled, "your dead ass is gonna get the captain a medal and a promotion."

"We got this shit wrong, man," said Scholar. "We shouldn't be shooting VC – we should be shooting that fucker Theodore. He's the one's gonna get us killed."

"There it is, man," said Gull.

Eventually, the complaints died down as they all fought off fatigue and the insects and leeches that dropped from the leaves around them. Above, a brace of birds clattered into the sky as they passed, the noise making a few of the jumpy New Guys stumble in fright. The sound eased away, leaving the soft, exotic clicks and whoops of a foreign woodland. Ahead of Scholar, Ryan's radio aerial bobbed and whipped through the foliage. Hissing voices emerged from the radio then quickly lost their battle with the trill of native wildlife. Green clad men draped in buckles and straps and pouches clutched their guns tightly, breathing as quietly as possible, every sense concentrated on the jagged and hostile greenery around them.

"I sincerely hope this is gonna be a walk in the sun," whispered

Ratman, his voice just audible over Lightning's shoulder. Ratman had reason to feel that way – he'd sent home a playing card every week he was out here, from a new deck. Now he only had Spades left.

"No sweat, m'man," Lightning said softly, without a trace of humour, "I got a feelin' here. Trust me." It was true. Lightning had developed a sort of gook radar. You could tell when trouble was coming your way – something in the atmosphere, like approaching storm clouds.

An FNG had bunched up on them. Lightning didn't know his name.

"I heard a guy on base say we were sure to hit some trouble today," the kid said.

Ratman glared at him. "Get the fuck outta my face, freshmeat. You go diddy-bopping into a landmine, you do it alone," he growled.

The kid fell back, an expression of hurt all over his face. They were just Fucking New Guys. They got in the way, fucked up and got short-timers wasted.

There was no point getting to know them. Like a stranger on the street, they'd probably never be seen again. It was better for them to die now, before they'd invested anything, seen the things that made you salty.

A little later the patrol halted. The point man had found a poorly concealed pit trap. After consulting the CO on the radio, and warning them all to be on their guard for more of the punji pits or other traps, Lieutenant Randall ordered them to continue.

Randall was okay. A Louie who'd put in some time and knew what he was doing. He could even read a map properly – more than the last shit-heel they'd been assigned. And he was known to cut the men some slack now and again, as long as it wouldn't harm his career. But around the other officers, Randall became a hard-ass.

The trees trailed off, leading to an area of dykes and paddies, and a small clutch of homes further on. The villagers weren't expecting them – the animals trotted around untethered. In single file, tense and wary, the soldiers passed between the wooden hootches. A mamasan balancing a huge bundle of sticks on her shoulder averted her gaze and scurried away for the safety of her home. An old man stared, face carefully blank.

This wasn't a Zippo raid; there'd be no burning today. Just passing through. Even so, Randall ordered a few grunts to shuffle through some randomly picked hootches, just so he could say he'd done his job. They'd go in, kick a few things over, prod stuff with their bayonets and leave. It was called winning the hearts and minds of the people. The peasants would just be glad that the interlopers hadn't shot a couple of their animals for fun.

The tension after finding the booby trap was bad enough. Even standing still was an effort, with adrenaline running overtime to fuel your heightened senses. But while the men searched the hootches, the tension tightened a couple of notches. One gunshot would be all it took for the whole platoon to erupt in a mixture of raw panic and raw aggression.

Lightning scoured everything in his field of vision – the bedraggled villagers, the wood and thatch huts, the scattered baskets and containers, the nervous animals, the paddy dikes that could act as cover for snipers. Then he examined everything once more, and continued this cycle until the search was finished and they continued on their way.

They halted a little way outside the ville, in a stand of bamboo thicket and trees, while the Lt reported in on the radio.

"Okay, listen up!" he shouted, after conferring on the handset, "We'll chow down here." He sounded as weary as Lightning felt. The nagging tension wouldn't go away. The platoon was like a group of hens in a fox's den.

Lightning pushed a tired head into his hands. His temples ached, his body was weary, his skin chafed and sore where pack straps and clothes abraded it.

A strange kind of madness swam around inside him. An oil and water mix of pity and hate. He pitied the poor farmers in the ville they'd passed through. They were without shoes, without anything but toil and harassment from patrols like this one. And yet he hated them. Hated them enough to empty his M-16 magazine into each and every gap-toothed, wizened face because they knew the people who'd set the booby traps, maybe even set some themselves. The same labour that went into raising their crops could have gone into priming and burying the salvaged 105mm artillery shell that had blown Voodoo Man apart. He was here to protect these people from

113

their own countrymen, and yet they helped the VC. There was a shocking revelation in there somewhere, and right now, Lightning didn't want to probe it. His head swam and his body twitched inside his skin. The sweat that beaded on his body wasn't only caused by the heat.

Letting himself fall into sitting position on the ground, Lightning shucked his pack and began rummaging for his C-rations, anger making his actions terse and violent. Scholar had been right. Captain Theodore was dangling them out here as bait, waiting for the willing enemy to come along and snap them up. Then Theodore would blow the area to shit with arty and airstrikes and come along and count the dead VC when the area was safe. A good count was all that mattered. Fuck the GIs who had to live this shit.

"Aw, fuck," he complained, opening a small tin of food. "Beans and motherfuckers. Wanna swap?" he asked Ratman.

Ratman gave him the finger and tucked into his own chow.

Tight-lipped, he avoided the gazes of the crashed out grunts and began the business of making and lighting a stove for coffee. He stared over at Ratman, who was running his finger around the empty can and licking it, not a care in the world.

Lightning was staring into the murky boiling water when the freshmeat came over.

"Hi," said the kid, a young brother with acne scars and unruly, tufted hair.

Lightning nodded but said nothing.

"I wanted to say sorry. For earlier I mean. I jus' wanna do things right, you know? I don't wanna get my ass shot off over here."

"Happens to us all," Lightning said sullenly.

"Not if I can help it, man. I wanna watch 'n' learn."

"You do that, freshmeat."

"My name's Cooper."

"I don't wanna know your name."

Ratman threw himself down beside Lightning. His gaze took in Cooper and passed over. "Got me some peanut butter and crackers," he said, "want some?"

"I don't know how you eat that shit," Lightning grumped.

"Why's everyone so shitty to us new guys?" whined the FNG.

114

Ratman looked up from spreading peanut butter with his finger. "This ain't kindergarten, man. You fuck up out here an' you die, maybe take one of us with you. We don't want that to happen."

"So why don't we get us some advice? No one tells us nothin'."

"You're gettin' OJT," said Ratman. Lightning smiled faintly.

"Say what?" asked Cooper.

"On-the-Job-Training." Ratman sucked peanut butter off his fingers and grinned.

A sudden flurry of weapons locked and loaded prompted a reflex reaction among the entire platoon. Coffee and rations hit the floor and weapons were quickly snatched up from the damp ground.

Lightning saw the cause of the commotion at the same time as the sentries did. He grabbed his rifle as the three Vietnamese peasants came into view, threading their way along the trail towards the men. Freshmeat, a beat behind the others, followed suit, head darting around like a rat sniffing danger.

It just looked like an old mamasan, a girl and a child to Lightning. But he knew as well as any of the short-timers here that *everything* was your enemy in this fucking country. If buffaloes could fire guns, they'd put on black pyjamas and hide in trees.

The mamasan was dressed in black, with the obligatory conical straw hat. She carried a yoke across her shoulder, two large baskets balanced on either end. She halted as the sentries screamed hysterically in her direction to stop what she was doing and put her hands on her head. Lightning saw the girl wavering, ready to bolt, her mouth a little black hole of panic. The small boy, barefoot and dressed in a grubby pair of washed-out grey trousers and a raggy shirt of the same colour, clung to her leg.

The sentries, Lyle and Mason, roughly dragged the three closer. The old woman let loose a stream of Vietnamese, her face scrunched up like a wailing kid, showing what few blackened teeth she had. She staggered beneath the weight of her swinging baskets.

The GIs around Lightning were visibly relaxing, inch by inch, rifle muzzles slowly drooping in proportion to their lack of interest in the scene.

"We do nothing wrong!" the girl was protesting.

115

Mason dragged the woman's baskets from her back and cast them to the ground. The shuffling scene kicked up dust amongst the tangled backdrop of bamboo bush.

"Shut up!" Mason screamed at the girl, his face reddening, "You VC bitch!"

"No," said the girl, eyes wide, "No VC! VC numbah ten. No VC."

The mamasan held her hands together now in prayer.

"What you prayin' for? You got something to hide. Huh? Huh?"

"Oh, man," Ratman drawled, "Mason's on a roll."

Sergeant Lee stood and walked over. Everyone called him 'Dixie', or 'General' Lee, on account of the Southern flag stencilled on the front of his helmet. The motherfucker waddled around like he could out-John Wayne John Wayne. "What we got here, trooper?"

"Caught these fuckin' gooks sneakin' up on us, sarge."

"No. No sneak. Please. No VC." cried the girl. The boy at her side was howling now, the old woman babbling again.

"Shut the fuck up!" snapped Dixie.

No change.

"Shut up!" Mason shook the old woman and she fell to the floor. The girl went to her aid. The kid ran.

"He's running!"

The sight of a gook heading for the men got them moving. They parted like the Red Sea for Moses, canteens and weapons clattering.

"He's got a grenade!" one of the FNGs cried in panic.

Lightning saw no grenade, just a frightened, howling kid darting for the safety of the village.

Dixie got down on one knee. His M-16 came up and drummed three succinct shots. Stars of propellant bloomed from the muzzle. The boy popped open, rolled and tumbled from the three bullet slaps. The body hit the floor, legs and flaps of blood-soaked cloth flailing out. Then the kid lay still.

Dixie's M-16 muzzle smoked lazily as he lowered it. For a moment there was silence. A slight frown on Ratman's face, nothing on Lightning's. Freshmeat had his mouth open like he'd just seen a hippo ballet dance across the White House lawn.

The Lt was the first to move, joining Mason beside the girl.

Ryan trailed along behind him, his radio still lying on the ground, forgotten. He had an almost content look on his face.

With a strange squawk, the girl tried to run for the heap of blood, dust and hair that lay motionless on the path. Mason yanked her back. She collided against his body and seemed to sink into herself, issuing a series of strangled cries. The mamasan had her hand to her over-wide mouth, her eyes shining with pooling tears. She made a protracted keening noise in the back of her throat.

The Lt barked orders. "Ryan, check the body – carefully. Lyle, take two men, check the 360. Sergeant, let's see what these people brought with them."

Lightning stood, as did many of the other soldiers, waiting to see what else would transpire.

"Whew!" someone exclaimed, "That little fucker ain't gonna be pickin' no more pockets."

Lightning watched Dixie through narrowed eyes as he carefully peeled back the cloth covering one of the baskets.

"Looky here."

Despite himself, Lightning shuffled forward and craned to see inside. Dixie unsheathed his K-bar knife and poked around carefully. Eventually satisfied, he beamed.

"Anyone for a coke?" he said, tossing a bottle to the nearest soldier, who, reluctant to let go of his gun, stepped away and allowed the bottle to smash open on the dusty ground.

"Let's see..." he said hoisting a US army tin up to the light, "we got tinned peaches, franks..."

"The kid's clean," shouted Ryan.

"What's in this one," asked one of the FNGs. He bent over and pulled the cover from the other basket. The old woman watched, sobbing, unseeing. Lightning's body tensed, and his jaw began to mouth a warning, but the soldier brashly reached inside.

"Fuck! She's got *beers* in here man!" He pulled out a bottle and held it up like a trophy. "Tiger beer!"

"All right! Party down!" Hoots and catcalls.

"That kid wasn't doing anything!" Freshmeat said in a high voice, staring at the bloody body.

"Welcome to the 'Nam." mumbled Scholar, who'd wandered over to stand beside Lightning and take in the scene.

"He coulda been fuckin booby-trapped or anything, man,"

117

came Gull's voice, accompanied by the rattle of his M-60 ammo.

"There it is," stated his A-gunner, Sanchez.

Dixie approached the young girl who bucked in Mason's grip, tears flying from her face. "Where'd you get this stuff?"

She shook her head, mouth open in silent anguish.

"What I wanna know, man," said a vociferous member of the congregation, "is how comes we gotta eat shitty peanut butter while the fucking slopes got peaches and beer and shit?"

"Right on."

"Hey, pass me a beer."

"Fuckin' gooks. We're dying for them while they eat peaches."

One marine began to work on the tin with his opener. He was soon joined by a crowd, dipping fingers into the can and slurping fruit, juice running down their chins.

Gull slapped Lightning on the shoulder. "Time for dessert!" He strode forward, calling for his share of the peaches. Sanchez trotted along behind him.

"You steal this stuff?" Dixie demanded of the girl.

Mamasan tried to rise, then sank to her knees, sobbing, as Dixie made to stop her. Ryan came over and stood close, scowling down at her.

"No... No steal," wailed the girl, "GI friend give..."

"She's fuckin' lying man. They're VC. Gonna feed their gook friends in the jungle. Ain't that right, mama?" Ryan nudged the old woman with his knee.

As though on cue, the mamasan waddle-crawled towards the boy's body, wailing, hands slapping the earth. "Where the fuck are you going?" Ryan demanded, yanking her by the collar.

"They're probably hungry after setting booby traps all day."

The old woman's sobbing rose to a demented, hoarse shout, and she struggled in Ryan's grip to reach the bundle of bloody clothing further up the path.

Dixie barked, "Soldier! Shut her up for Christ's sake!"

Ryan unslung his rifle. Everyone stood and watched. He brought it to his shoulder. A group were passing out beers, ignoring the weeping woman at the wrong end of an M-16.

Lyle and the two scouts returned, staring with interest at the scene. Lt Randall turned and walked over to receive their report.

118

Ratman jostled forward for a beer, grabbed one and thrust one towards Lightning. He lowered his gun and took it with his free hand, his gaze still on Ryan. Freshmeat jostled past towards the baskets.

"Oh man, beer is good."

"Fuckin' A!"

Crack. The gun went off and the old woman sprawled in the dirt, a great swath of her clothing torn away to expose macerated flesh and nobbles of her spine. Lightning didn't even flinch; it was all so fucking inevitable.

Dixie glared at the still form, caught Lightning's gaze for the briefest of intervals. His hand went to his mouth, his eyes dark and calculating.

"Let's have us a piece of VC poontang," he said quietly, and reached out and tore away the distraught girl's blouse.

"No... No do this GI!" she kicked and fought, fresh tears squeezing from her red raw eyes.

"All right!" cried Mason, grabbing her arms and giggling. Lightning watched. She had small breasts. How long since he'd had a woman? Nothing going in the hospital. Whores in the field had God knew what diseases. He wondered where the Lt was while all this was happening. He scanned the perimeter, and saw the Lt and a couple of others over by a tree in the distance. Randall looked over, then consciously looked away. It had been a hard day in the field, they'd captured VC sympathisers. It was the spoils of war. Chalk three VC down to the body count.

"Open her fucking legs!" A wild animal's growl.

There was no shortage of volunteers. No questions. Even the freshmeat was looking for a better position to see splayed female flesh. They were animals. They were all animals. And Lightning was an animal too. That's what they did out here – hunted and killed. Kill or be killed, Voodoo Man would tell you that. They'd been on the receiving end for so long; it was time to even the score.

Lightning was aware of someone beside him. He turned, and met Scholar's gaze. His drawn reflection stared back from the lenses of Scholar's glasses. The eyes behind the frames were haunted but calculating. Their gaze locked for seconds before Scholar stepped forward like a damned man to join the others.

The girl's cries were lost in the general hubbub. She was stretched between two groups of marines like a pig on a spit, arms over her head, legs straight out and baggy trousers yanked to her knees. Lightning felt a rush of lust. Part of him knew all this was wrong, but that part only created a burning in his gut that fuelled his lust.

No one questioned what was going on here. The part of them that existed to stay alive, to avoid the booby traps and shoot anyone who fucked with them, didn't care. It was a shadow person inside, teased out by the call of the wild. They were a trained pack of these shadow creatures, all knowing their place in the mechanics of the kill. Lightning wanted to join them, he wanted to stop them, he wanted to die.

They'd got her pinned to the floor now. Lightning stepped forward, jostled by his neighbours. Dixie was pumping it to her – finished quickly. Someone else was there to take his place. Lightning saw the girl's twisted, agonised face.

They were all alike, these gooks; they wanted nothing but to harm you. He'd been violated back at the temple. His old self killed stone-dead, and the only way to resurrect himself was to avenge his violation, blast out the intruder on the wave of hate that had built inside him.

"Line up, man, stop fighting! You'll all get your turn!" said Dixie.

They all did. Lightning lay on top of her strangely cold, tight body, mashed his face against hers and felt her icy little tears on his skin. She breathed a word as he came. It sounded like "Why?"

He pulled away, hoisting up his fatigues. Someone else bulled in, pushing him across towards the bodies of the old woman and the kid. His pumped-up body suddenly collapsed back into itself. The sickness hit him, a painful punch up from his stomach and into his throat. He staggered for the edge of the trail.

The first heave lodged in his throat, choking him. He could hear the hoots and catcalls, small and seemingly insignificant.

His legs would no longer hold his weight. He tottered a little further into the undergrowth, propping himself against a tree. "No," he rasped.

If he'd had the energy he would have cried out louder than

120

ever in his entire life. Louder than when he'd seen Voodoo Man blasted apart like a blood-filled balloon.

But no one was listening anyhow. They'd finished with the girl. She lay in a ragged heap on the floor, unmoving even when a couple of them kicked her. They pulled the rest of her clothing away, dragging and flinging it through the dust.

Everything was unreal – the group of combat-uniformed men who howled and tore at the naked body of the girl like wolves, the blood and the dust and the taste of vomit in his mouth. He suddenly felt very alone, an alien in a land of madness and death.

The sergeant swung his M-16 like he was on parade, and blasted three quick shots into the girl's inert form.

Beside him, one of the young FNG's gave a rebel yell. "Fuck, man. Did you see that?"

Ryan spoke, his voice low and spiteful. "No more boom boom for mamasan." His face was wolfish; his slow motion smile showed sharp little canine teeth.

Lightning wiped the bad taste from his mouth and half-fell, half-sat on the dusty ground.

"Fucking gooks!" Someone took a stamp at the dead body. Followed by a kick from someone else. They were all animated, like wild cartoons, red faces pulled into hate masks. "Teach these slimy fuckers to dig punji pits!"

Mason pulled out a long bowie knife. Excited, like a kid at Holiday time, he rushed toward the girl's bloody body. His blond hair was dust matted and spiked.

"Move! I'm gonna souvenir me a VC ear!" He bundled into the crowd, grabbing and sawing.

The freshmeat stood away off, fumbling with his pack. Lightning watched him produce a camera and begin taking photos of the dead old woman. As he raised the camera, her arm moved, brushing feebly against the ground. Freshmeat jerked back, shock on his face.

Another FNG pulled up beside him. "This one's still alive man!"

"Hey, lemme shoot her!"

"No way, this one's mine." He began to pull the K-bar from his utility belt.

Lightning's hands went to his face. His skin was as cold as

121

death. One minute he bubbled with hate and wanted to re-join the ritual cleansing atrocity, the next he was frozen in disbelief, self-hatred and revulsion. His body felt like a vat of curdling liquids and fats. He was a hardened killer, he was a frightened child.

Standing, he began to walk slowly through the carnage, the butt of his '16 dragging in the dirt. The girl's body was no longer recognisable as human, and the hunched, ghoulish figures of his comrades were hacking at it, taking away hunting trophies. "I want her titties!"

Ratman crouched over her body, knife in hand, grinning at Lightning. Lightning was sure that Ratman couldn't really see him.

Beyond the kicked up dust and gore, the forest stood silently, watching without judgement. A misty fog seemed to be gathering around the foliage, tendrils of it drifting toward Lightning like welcoming arms.

With trepidation, Lighting left his platoon behind and marched into the inviting jungle.

Steve Byrne is the author of Phoenix, *a dark horror novel set during the Vietnam War. If you enjoy 'Piranha', look it up on Amazon. Steve has recently returned to writing after a gruelling tour of duty in the urban wastelands of the West Midlands.*

THE BALLAD OF BAILEY BLONDE
by Marc Sorondo

Bailey pushed her blonde hair out of her eyes to better watch him: the way his mouth moved to form each word, the way he cocked his head between verses, the way his fingers plucked and strummed the strings of his guitar.

All of his songs were about pain and loss and death. His voice wailed and his guitar wept. His songs were the evolution of the blues, a soundtrack to despair for a modern age.

She loved him. In spite of, or possibly because of, the pain that filled his music, she found him beautiful. His hair was long and wavy brown and his face was an angel's. His voice, though, was old and gravelly, aged by smoking too many cigarettes and drinking too much bourbon.

His name, he said, was Johnny Destiny. In his music, he was the angel of death.

> My name is Destiny, baby
> Everyone meets me in the end…

Bailey had followed his progress in the area from bar to bar, where he played to crowds of people who couldn't possibly appreciate him. Once in a while she'd spot a face in the crowd and she would see recognition, recognition of his genius maybe, or, more likely, recognition of a type of pain that they shared with him, perhaps the loss of an old friend or the disappearance of a former love.

Bailey ordered another Jack and coke and watched his face while he sang. There was a slight, melancholy smile there.

> I watched your mother crying
> 'Cause she knew I stole you away

123

I saw that she was dying
'Cause she knew you'd done the same

After his last song, one called "The Damned," about the killing of a rapist, she approached him at the bar.

She'd imagined doing it for weeks now, since the first time she saw him and heard him. Tonight she'd finally had enough to drink to do it.

"I love your songs," she said as she slid up to the bar next to him.

He met her eyes with his, and she saw that his were the colour of black coffee.

"Well, thank you very much," he said, a distinct southern lilt to his rough voice.

"Where do you get your inspiration?" she asked.

The bartender placed a glass in front of Johnny and poured four fingers of bourbon into it.

"Life is full of inspiring things," he said. He picked up his drink and motioned, with a nod of his head and a flash of his eyes, to a row of booths away from the bar.

She led him over and slid into the booth furthest from the din of the crowded bar.

"I've seen you before," he said with a wink that may or may not have been intentional and a smile that was equal parts jaded and boyish. "You were there when I played at Ray's on route 102."

She blushed and drank two swallows of her Jack and coke. "Yeah. I've been going to all your gigs since you got into the area. I love your music."

He lifted his glass as if in cheers and poured half the drink into his mouth. He looked at his glass and then hers and, with a flourish of his hand, motioned for the waitress to bring them each another.

"You're too pretty to like music that's so sad," he said.

"It's still beautiful. You capture it and…it's sort of raw and compelling, but beautiful at the same time."

"That's no talent on my part, I assure you," he said. He downed the rest of his bourbon. "It's just the subject matter."

"There's more to it than that," she argued.

The waitress came and placed the drinks in front of them. Destiny slipped a bill out from his shirt pocket and into her hands.

"I write about what I know," he said as the waitress turned and left.

"You know death?"

"First song I ever wrote," he said with a nod, "was about my parents."

"They died?" she asked, immediately wincing and feeling stupid because the answer was so obvious.

He nodded solemnly. "They were murdered when I was fourteen."

She covered her mouth with a hand and gasped, "Oh my god… I'm so sorry."

He closed his eyes and sang:

> When I see you next
> Don't be mad
> 'Cause the life I've chosen
> It really ain't so bad
>
> Just a wandering fool
> But I want to make you proud
> Just hard to hear your words
> With your screams still so loud

"You don't think they'd be proud you chose to be a musician?" Bailey asked.

"Something like that."

She loved his pain when she thought it just part of some created persona. Now that she knew it was real, that he wrote about death because it had touched him so intimately, she loved him all the more.

After two more rounds, they left. She'd invited him back to her place for one last round, and he'd agreed with another of those contradictory smiles.

"Where will you play next?" she asked him once they'd gotten into her car.

He shrugged. "Don't know. It's probably getting to be time I moved on again."

"Oh," she said, her disappointment clearer than she'd intended it to be.

"Don't be sad. I've got to keep moving. It's part of my music. Moving and seeing things and writing about them."

"Why don't you record your music? Make an album?" Bailey asked.

Johnny shook his head. "Not ready yet. Someday I'm going to do just that... but I haven't written enough songs yet."

"I've heard you play a lot of different songs. How many are yours?"

"All of them," he said.

"All of them?" she laughed for a second. "How many do you need?"

"Once I settle, I don't think I'll be able to write any more. I have to write enough for the rest of my life."

They had the round of drinks they'd agreed upon and then, as she'd hoped, they made love.

She wanted to use her body to soothe his pain. She wanted to give him a reason to stay. She wanted him to write songs about her. After all, she loved him.

Once they'd finished, they laid next to each other in the dark of her bedroom. He seemed content with the silence, but she found it saturated with potential: that he'd leave, that she'd never convey her feelings for him, that down the road he wouldn't even remember her.

She laid in the darkness and smelled him, the scent of sweat and bourbon and something else, something uniquely him.

She couldn't bear it. The thought of him leaving terrified her, but not nearly as much as the thought that she would let him leave without even trying. She sought her voice and found that the Jack Daniel's effect on it had faded.

She felt despair in the pit of her stomach.

He half rolled over to her and asked, "Do you mind if I smoke?"

"I think I love you," she replied.

In the dark she could see that he smiled, then she heard a low chuckle come from him. She couldn't decipher the meaning of either, couldn't tell if he was happy because he loved her as well or laughing at her stupidity.

Then she felt his hands on her, running slowly up her torso and over her breasts.

She smiled at his touch.

He wrapped his hands around her throat and squeezed. Her eyes, opened wide in shock, caught glints of light coming in the window and shone.

He squeezed and her delicate mouth, one he'd found was so soft, opened into a chasm, one through which no scream could escape and no breath could enter.

Her body thrashed. Her hands beat against him. But she quickly grew weak. There was no struggling against him. He was Destiny.

He watched the life in her run out.

Every death, he knew, was like a sonnet, marked by a steady rhythm and building to the final, supremely final, rhyming couplet that was the last gasping breath or the final desperate thought before there was nothing.

He set that poetry to music.

He watched her eyes and saw when, with a last spectacular glimmer, the life left them. Then he let her go.

He rolled over and turned on the lamp on the table beside the bed. Then he reached down and pulled a silvery cigarette case and a beaten-up notebook from his guitar case.

He pulled a hand-rolled cigarette from the case and lit it. He took a few thoughtful drags before opening the notebook.

It was already half full of other songs… other lives. Once it was full, he'd reveal himself to the world, and then he'd be famous. He'd go down in history for the way his songs capture life and death.

He flipped to a blank page and wrote, "Bailey Blonde," before taking a few more pulls of his cigarette. Then:

'Twas the truth that killed my lover

I just took the blame
It wasn't me she really loved
Just the songs that I sang

She gave all herself to me
But the road called my name
Said she'd die if I left her
And I said, Baby, that's my game...

Marc Sorondo lives with his wife and children in New York. He loves to read, and his interests range from fiction to comic books, physics to history, oceanography to cryptozoology, and just about everything in between. He's a long time student and occasional teacher. For more information, go to MarcSorondo.com.

OLD BONES
by Shannon Quinn

Roger promised to visit his girl as long as he didn't have to wear the bonnet. He has to draw the line somewhere. He hears her small steps, her breath coming in excited gasps. He sees her tangled brown curls in the distance. She is tripping along behind her mother.

Roger waits on the front stoop, soaking the last of the summer heat from the cement steps.

The girl's eyes find him, "Hello Kitty Cat!" She is slapping him repeatedly on the head. Roger assumes she believes she is petting him. Her mother is fumbling with a set of keys,

"I said be gentle with that thing. You probably shouldn't even be touching it, it could have rabies or fleas." She mashes a key into the lock and opens the door. The girl holds Roger up, gripping him under his front legs so that he dangles inelegantly.

"He's coming to my party." She bolts upstairs with Roger held out in front of her, swinging like a pendulum.

Mr. Eisman hears the mother's clattering heels on the stairs above him… heels attached to feet attached to curved lean legs. He purses his mouth. He knows he mustn't let those kinds of thoughts into his head. He must stop all of his thinking and be still.

Early this morning he'd run into the mother as she was leaving for work. Her pulpy red mouth chewed out words asking him to look in on the girl during the evening, "unless it would be too much trouble." His tongue had retreated and plugged the back of his throat like a garden slug. He'd had to nod yes instead of speak. Speaking to women who weren't girls was highly unpleasant. Women were loud and their words were far too slippery.

Upstairs, Roger, a plastic frog, a mangy stuffed rabbit and the girl are all sitting in a circle. Roger is wearing a yellow bonnet trimmed with lace. His girl is pouring tea and keeping up an animated one-sided conversation. In the light of day there is no hint of the night terrors.

Yesterday evening Roger climbed up the fire escape and slipped in through her window. He had felt her whimpers right through the ceiling and deep into his bones. The terrors whispered his name as sure as they trapped her in her sleep. She sees a dark roiling sky, flooded with the milky colour of cataracts... the girl wonders to herself, who stole all of the colour... just as thundering grey emaciated bodies hurtle themselves toward her, eyes rolled back into their heads. Roger pushed himself up against her chest, purred loudly and patted at her face with his paw.

She flailed awake, throwing Roger off of the bed. She sat upright and still for a moment before she carefully pulled back the sheets she had peed in, bundled them up and hid them in the back of her closet. Then she curled up on the floor with a blanket. From under the bed Roger watched to make sure she slid back through the folds of sleep, not getting snared in roiling skies.

Roger is twenty. Twenty is old for a cat. Twenty is old to be wearing a bonnet. His girl is so young. Special. She sees what the others cannot: the shadows in the night, the extraordinary brightness of day, the weight of air, the thought of a breeze. One blink of her tiny eyelids freezes time and the second blink frees it.

He hopes he'll be gone when it happens, when she sloughs off her childhood as all of them must. Her soul, snuggling against the infinite, will be tugged ever so slightly away. Everything will be set in motion, too quickly and without warning. It might be at recess or while hiding in a closet or sitting beside a stranger on a bus. No one can ever predict the exact moment that childhood evaporates. Roger has seen it so often, this time he'd rather be gone when it happens.

He excuses himself from the tea party. It's past his naptime. He gingerly navigates his way down the fire escape. Once inside the apartment he can see Mr. Eisman behind his curtained partition that he uses as a bedroom wall. The shop is a dark place. The lamplight coming from beside Mr. Eisman's cot elongates a ghoulish skeletal frame against the wall. It's his naptime also.

Roger waits for the creak, then the settling of the cot. The main room of the shop is full of Mr. Eisman's dusty supplies. He used to make homemade medicine but all his customers died. Tucked off to the far left corner, directly across from the window, is a gloriously overstuffed and dented armchair that seems out of place in Eisman's orderly world. Roger ambles towards the chair, passing the shelves of dried out poultices and jars of dark mucky liquid, mustard seeds, mushrooms… it was the mushrooms that had once made Roger very ill after he'd had a small nibble… and he'd seen the queerest things.

There was also a time when he'd knocked over a bottle that held a gallbladder. He hadn't been able to resist and had gobbled it up and then hid for a week to avoid any repercussions. A small bottle of cat whiskers used to be kept on the same shelf, and when Roger saw it running low he always made himself scarce.

Roger is at the armchair now and silently leaps up, curling himself into a ball. His skin is beginning to relax when a loud thwack prickles his fur and his back arches before he jumps off the chair.

Mr. Eisman has launched a magazine at him, but thankfully his aim is poor.

"Charlie, you stay off that damn chair. Bad Cat. Bad!"

Roger does not understand why Mr. Eisman has insisted on calling him Charlie for the past eighteen years, nor does he understand why he isn't allowed to sleep on the unused chair.

Roger settles on the vent under the window, which has its own pleasures. Roger had spent two lean years on the street before arriving at Eisman's door, with ribs poking through dull fur and half an ear missing. Eisman had put down a dish of milk and opened a can of sardines. Roger had finished them, curled up on a worn blanket and felt for the first time the pleasure of a full belly and a deep uninterrupted sleep.

An uninterrupted sleep is eluding Eisman this afternoon. His sharp elbows pinch the thin mattress. A blanket is tucked in just under his armpits. The long grey curls of hair on his chest stand straight up, embarrassed, as if they've been caught doing something shameful. Pale blue veins thread his arms. His ribs are well defined. Mother had always told him a good physique meant being able to count your ribs. His nylon socks have lost their elasticity and pool by his ankles. Thick ropy veins work their way up his shins, stopping at knees caked white with rough dead skin.

Roger gently leaps back onto the armchair, confident he will have at least an hour's peace. He knows Eisman's habits better than the man himself does and this is what troubles Roger now, he's never before felt this darkness ticking away in Eisman's head.

It seems worse to him that Eisman might not even be aware of it himself.

From his rickety cot the old man starts to slide, almost falling into rest only to catch himself before sleep hits. Mother called him a nervous sleeper. He knows if he waits long enough, and thinks only good thoughts, sleep will come and swallow him.

Roger is restless. Usually he can block the tics and noises of all the fragments that rush through Eisman's head. But today he can't. The invitation from the mother of his little girl has started something... something Roger can't stop, something the base of his tail tells him is awful. This morning he'd heard her knocking... asking... *tonight, would he mind... she hated to impose, she hadn't foreseen...*

Then came Mr. Eisman's slow bob of his turtle like head, *not a problem... there would be no inconvenience.*

Mr. Eisman had been very pleased. At last. He wanted to know what that little girl up there dreamed of. He longed for it, after so many years of manipulating, eradicating the illness in other people's minds and bodies. He just wanted to lean in close enough to smell those clean healthy breaths that escaped in the night, watch her eyelids flutter, wonder about the visions fluttering across her nocturnal landscape. Why shouldn't the child share this with him? He deserved it. Hadn't he earned it? Soon enough she would turn into one of those women with the slippery words.

Roger is standing at the foot of Mr. Eisman's cot. The smell of the shop is thick with dank sweat. Roger usually heads to the fire escape at times like this, but instead he slinks slowly back to the main room... and then catches himself...it must have been five years since he's slunk anywhere, but he feels supple and his body is easy, as if he's been allowed new muscles and stronger bones... how wonderful. He sits bright eyed... he can hear mice in the next house over. His vision that had slowly grown milky is now pristinely clear.

Mr. Eisman opens his eyes, his mind stinging from an unsettling sleep. He shuffles to the bathroom to start his wash. He turns the tap on, hot, scalding hot, and waits for his claw-foot tub to fill. He looks in the tin mirror he has tacked above the sink. Stubble. Grey stubble. He brushes foam across his chin and with a dollar store razor hacks unsuccessfully at the afternoon's growth. His tub is almost full. He has a little wooden stand beside it with reading material, lavender soaps like his mother used to have, bath salts and his radio. He listens to the oldies stations. He bought the radio

132

second-hand, it was a luxury that didn't really suit him but the price had been good. He tunes into his station and steps into the tub, easing himself into the steam, feeling the slow burn wash over him.

The man in the pawnshop had slapped the radio saying, "They don't make them like this anymore!" Mr. Eisman knew this to be true; it was very much like one his mother and father had owned. They'd turn it on every Sunday night, after their roast beef dinner and dance around the living room. Father's hands would be on mother's waist and they'd be laughing, knocking into the furniture. Eisman would make himself smile—a small hard smile. He mustn't appear angry. Their dancing, daddy's hands on mommy made him invisible. It was as if mommy couldn't see him. And he couldn't have that.

He sinks further into the tub. The Mills brothers are singing,

> "I'm gonna buy a Paper Doll that I can call my own
> A doll that other fellows cannot steal."

Eisman wiggles his toes and in a thin warble joins in, off-key.

> "I'd rather have a Paper Doll to call my own
> Than have a fickle-minded real live girl."

He hears a voice, the *mother's* voice.

"Mr. Eisman?"

Good god she's not going to enter is she? Had she heard him singing?

"Occupied. I'm occupied."

"I'm so sorry"—she's yelling from outside the door, he relaxes just a little.

"It's just I need to leave early. She's had her dinner and is ready for bed, she'll tuck herself in, if you could just check on her every now and then."

"Of course, yes, yes, not a problem."

"Good night then."

"Good night."

As she clatters away a new song comes on the radio, Eisman's dry lips crack into a tiny smile.

133

"Irene goodnight, Irene goodnight."

The door separates Roger from the mother. He is pushing himself into it, wishing he could worry it open, wrap himself around her ankles, trip her. Make her stop.

"Goodnight Irene, goodnight Irene
I'll see you in my dreams."

Eisman is humming to the radio.

He must get himself out of the tub, apply some lotion, some aftershave. He didn't expect to be rushed.

Roger is in the washroom staring at Mr. Eisman as he does a final scrub of his armpits. Roger is sad...or he assumes he is feeling something close to sadness, he may not have been fond of Eisman, but the man had been kind to him.

Eisman spots Roger and coos absentmindedly, "Charlie, Charlie, Charlie what am I going to do with you? Always in the way you are, yes, you're a bad cat, a naughty cat."

Roger jumps up onto the small table beside the tub.

"Oh have I got myself a swimmer cat. Are you going to start taking your – "

Mr. Eisman doesn't finish. Roger has stealthily and smoothly pushed his body up against the old heavy radio, dumping it into the tub.

The bathroom fuse blows.

For a moment Mr. Eisman is vibrating, eyes bulging, mouth open as if he has something he must say. Then he is still.

Roger jumps onto the fire escape and makes his way up the stairs.

He tumbles in through his girl's window. Not as strong as he was earlier.

She is sitting up with a fresh sheet over her head, holding a flashlight, and having a discussion with whom Roger assumes can only be her stuffed rabbit and plastic frog. He gingerly jumps up onto the bed. She feels him right away.

"Kitty!" an arm shoots out from under the blanket and drags

him under.

"Now our sleepover will be a really big one!" She's swaddling him with a towel.

"We have to be good and say our prayers. Now I lay me down to sleep."

Roger likes the warmth of her breath against the top of his head.

"I pray the Lord my soul to keep. If I should die."

She turns him slightly so they are nose to nose.

"Before I wake..." Roger relishes the sweetness of her breath and steals just a tiny bit for himself. "I pray the Lord..."

And only as a child can she slips unguardedly and effortlessly though the gates of sleep.

He stays with her for an hour, riding the slow waves of her ribcage then quietly slides out from under the sheets. He doesn't want her to feel him grow cold. He takes the fire escape, this time each step is a labour. Old bones.

He slips back in through the window, and as his paws make contact with the floor he winces. He eyes the forbidden armchair, summons the last of his energy, leaps into it, turns three times and settles down with a deep sigh. Back home. He and Eisman.

His sigh rattles just a little and catches.

Twenty is very old.

Shannon Quinn *lives in Toronto, Canada with three cats who may or may not be plotting to kill her. Her writing has appeared in literary journals in Ireland, Germany, United States, Australia and Canada.*

AN HONEST WOMAN'S CHILD
by Jo Thomas

Kier hung out the window, clinging to the shutter he'd just opened, and watched the people who moved around the first square-cut stones that had been laid out the day before. He couldn't decide if this new thing was good or bad.

"What is it?" Mum asked.

Don't know, Kier thought. He breathed out heavily through his nose, because some kind of response was expected.

"Let me see," she said as she pulled him back in.

Kier hmphed and willed the day back into something like the usual texture. If he tried, he could pretend the strange thing happening diagonally across the street did not exist.

"Oh, it's that Arch," Mum said. "The monument they're putting on the new avenue."

She said more but Kier didn't listen to the words, just let the sounds flow in one ear and out the other like the stream under the wooden bridge. He didn't want to know about the things that changed.

Because it was what he did every morning, he took the chamber pot and emptied it in the washroom. He had to do it now because Mum shouted at him if he returned it when a visitor was with her.

On the way back up, the pot was light enough for him to hold it with one hand and trail the other along the hand-rail. It was worn with use and familiarity like Kier's days and he liked them both that way. Where there were differences in his days, they had the subtlety of wood-grain. As comforting and soothing a texture against his mind as the hand-rail itself was against his hand.

He liked the day-grain. He liked the days when Mum put aside her visitors and took Kier to the market to buy their food. He liked the days when Mum took him to the gardens of a nearby villa, where she met the woman who gave him an apple so that she could

136

spend the day with Mum alone. He liked to eat the apple standing in the middle of the wooden bridge, watching the stream flash over the rocks below.

It was best to touch these things lightly though, because there were some normal differences he didn't like. Less pleasant, like a splinter or nail sticking from the rail, and just as unexpected no matter how prepared he thought he was - like being ambushed by the shop-owners' children on the way from the courtyard to the street, or the children from rooms higher up the tenement throwing things at him.

Some differences didn't match life's hand-rail at all. Like the big fire, when several neighbouring blocks were destroyed. Sometimes these things were good and sometimes they were bad, though Kier and Mum didn't always agree which was which. The fire had been beautiful despite the piercing screams from those people that ran from the burning buildings.

This new thing didn't match. It was a change.

Every day that wasn't a market or a garden day, Kier was pushed out of the room with a chunk of oil-soaked bread and a piece of hard yellow cheese. Most mornings, he passed the first visitor as he sway-stepped down the stairs. Typically, they ignored him or called him a tenement brat.

Most days he lay in the courtyard and stared up at the sky, watching the clouds move across the small patch of blue. It wasn't interesting when there were no clouds at all or nothing but cloud. Some days, he tried to copy the patterns, scratching them into the gravel with a stick.

That day, he couldn't watch the clouds because the stones across the road – the Arch, Mum had said – nagged at him. He could feel the strangers in his head, knew they were moving around making this new thing that didn't belong. He wanted things to stay the same. He wanted the buildings that had been burnt away to be put back.

Kier sidled past the shop that made the ground floor of the tenement and up to the passageway that led out of the courtyard. He couldn't see the Arch.

"What're you doing there?" the grocer's wife asked.

Kier didn't answer. He was too busy taking the next step along the passageway – but it wasn't enough because he still couldn't see the men working. He couldn't until he had stepped out of the passageway and even taken an extra step to stand in the middle of the narrow street. A quarter-turn to his right brought them into view, still slightly hidden by the houses across the street.

"Get out the way!"

Someone shouted nearby and Kier flinched.

"Move, idiot!"

A hand grabbed him and pulled him backwards. He looked round, mouth open on an aggrieved grunt. It fell from his mouth, lost when he saw the grocer's wife. She wasn't looking at him.

"Sorry," she said, "The mother's just – you know, just an honest woman."

She shrugged and the shouting stopped.

It took Kier a full seven days to creep along the street, his hand trailing on the tenement's outside wall, and near enough to the Arch to get a decent view of the work the men did. He stood and watched with his eyes and mouth wide open. He watched the Arch rise over the new, wide road that passed through it. He gave the new avenue a cursory glance then watched the men who shaped the Arch. They moved backwards and forwards, chiselling at the stones, sticking them together, making shapes with their noise.

In another week he had crept close enough to put a shaking hand on an unattended stone flank. He stroked out lines he could see in his head, nothing to do with the edges of the individual stones but everything to do with how they stayed where they were.

"Hey! You!"

Kier jerked his hand back as if the Arch was too hot to touch any more. A rough hand grabbed at his shoulder and forced the turn Kier didn't dare make. It was the eyebrows he noticed, meeting together in a wriggly line that always came before people started shouting. He forced himself to look down at the moving mouth but the sounds made no sense. Fear had changed them into that familiar running, indecipherable stream of noise. He only noticed the tone, harsh like the stream was running fast over rocks. He swallowed and waited for the lips to stop moving, but the stranger shook him and demanded something.

Kier grunted, the only answer anyone ever expected of him. The stranger's lips moved again, his tone still rough. There was another shake. Then a pause.

"Well?"

Kier blinked, surprised the word had floated above the stream. "A – " he managed in response.

"What?" the stranger asked.

I came to look at the Arch, Kier thought, *to see how it works.* He pointed at the stones and grunted. He swallowed again and then croaked out, "Agh – argh – "

"You came to see the Arch?"

The tone had calmed, the rocks disappearing to allow smoother water through, more like the stream in the garden. Kier nodded.

"And what did you see?" the stranger asked. "What were you drawing on the stones?"

Kier grunted. *I don't know what it's called.*

"Show me," the man said and he let go of Kier's shoulder.

Kier, scared of what the man might to do, ran home.

Kier was trying to make his own arch from the small irregular stone chippings on the ground. The fragments wouldn't rest easily on each other and the fight to make them stay had Kier grunting. *Behave. Do* this. *Sit* here.

"Boy?"

Kier ignored the interruption. The call wouldn't be for him. No-one ever called for him. No-one ever called him "Boy".

"Boy!"

Kier continued to grunt at the stone chips. It was frustrating that they didn't listen and do as they were told.

"You have a talent, boy," the voice said from close by and Kier jumped, knocking the arch into a tiny ruin.

"Ner!" he said. *No!*

Hands appeared over his shoulder, picking up stones and making the ruin a jumbled mess. The hands looked like the ones that had grabbed him at the big Arch, and Kier realised the voice was like the one he'd heard before, too.

"Ner!" Kier said again and slapped at the hands.

The hands flew out of sight. "I'm just trying to help you!"

"Don't bother with her," the grocer's wife called.

Kier said "Ner!" again and covered his ears.

"She's touched and her mother has no time for her," the grocer's wife added.

"Her?" asked the other voice.

"Ner!" said Kier in answer. He didn't want to be a girl. Girls grew up to be women and had to have husbands or visitors.

"Her mother leaves her hair long and dresses her in infant's rags," said the grocer's wife.

"Ner!" said Kier again, shaking his head. He liked his hair and his vest.

"It's fine... boy," the other voice said and a hand touched his shoulder.

Kier shifted his shoulder out of the way but didn't move from over his pile of stones. He looked at the owner of the voice. Was it the man from the Arch, following him to punish him for drawing lines? The eyebrows had drawn together and looked like the ones he'd seen that other time. Kier shuffled his feet.

"Take me to your mother," the man said.

Kier didn't answer but the grocer's wife did. She laughed and said, "If you want the honest woman, she's two flights up, first door on the right. Don't think she's got a visitor right now."

Kier watched until the man disappeared into the darkness of the tenements, then looked down at his little ruin. He was disappointed that the man had turned out to be just another visitor. Kier had almost thought the man was here to see him.

He tried again to get the stones to balance. After the second collapse, he pushed the pile of stones away and ran up the stairs to his room. Perhaps the visitor had finished and would know how to make an arch out of the stone chips.

"You left me to become a whore? An honest woman?" Kier heard the man shout as he climbed the stairs.

They weren't the kind of words visitors usually used with Mum, so Kier crept up to the door to listen. The man had left it half-open and he could just see their shadows as they moved in the light from the window.

"You didn't want Kiera," Mum shouted, "You didn't want a girl. She wasn't good enough for you!"

"A girl can't learn to be an architect," the man said, almost too quietly to be heard. "Anyway, what have you won for hi – her? Is she going to grow up to be like her mother, nothing but a common whore?"

There was a sound like a loud clap and one shadow struck the other. "How dare you! How dare you come here and treat me like this! I was your wife."

"Was. You chose to leave me and take my... child with you."

"You didn't want her. You didn't want us."

"I saw the child at the Arch," the man said, quiet again.

A laugh as sharp as the shouting. "And that changed everything, did it?"

"He – The child has a talent for building," the man said, "Like my family."

"Kiera has a talent for nothing. She hasn't even got the brains to talk."

The larger shadow hunched over, well away from the smaller. "I had a brother like that."

"Then your brother was a damned idiot and useless!"

The smaller shadow also hunched.

"You stole h – her from me," the man said, a soft almost-whisper, "You stole my child from me."

"I didn't steal her, you didn't want her! You didn't want either of us! You just wanted your precious buildings."

There was a moment of silence and then Kier held his breath as the larger shadow stood over the smaller. "What is that supposed to mean?"

"You never had time for me. You were always more bothered about your precious buildings. I'll bet that Arch is one of yours, too."

"You're saying you slept with another man when we were married?"

Mum laughed. "Maybe you should talk to your current wife. She has the same problem. She even pays for an honest woman's company."

The shadows stilled again.

"Pardon?" the man said slowly and clearly.

But it seemed like Mum didn't hear because she spoke loudly. "How does that feel? To know you're so useless as a husband that your wife has to pay for an honest woman's gift? She gives Kiera apples, you know. Bribery so that the idiot girl will give us privacy in your gardens."

There was a pause and then Mum continued, "I make her scream. I make her call out. Do you know who she calls for? Me!"

"Shut your filthy mouth!"

"Does it hurt? To know I'm a better man to your wife than you will ever be? And I'm just a hired lover, a common whore?"

The larger shadow lashed out, arms reaching to the neck of the smaller.

"Bitch! Shut up!"

Mum made croaking sounds and the smaller shadow hit at the larger. Over a number of heartbeats, the smaller shadow stilled and slumped, then dropped altogether.

The door opened fully and the man was there, walking from the room. The man stopped in front of Kier and looked down at him.

"Why don't you come with me, boy?" the man asked. "I can show you how to build an arch."

Kier blinked up at the man. It was exactly what he wanted to ask for.

"And I always wanted a son," the man said.

"Muh?" asked Kier. *What about Mum?*

Jo Thomas *writes speculative fiction, tending towards dark fantasy. She has taken the advice "write what you know" to heart and, as a result, werewolves now turn up in the strangest places. (None were harmed in the writing of* 25 Ways To Kill A Werewolf *but friendly vets were pumped for advice.) To find out more about Jo, her pack of Hellhounds and her interest in swords along with the odd piece of fiction that doesn't contain werewolves, have a look at http://www.journeymouse.net/.*

ARTHUR'S CELLAR
by Anna Taborska

Arthur raced through the darkening forest, ignoring the branches that scratched him and the roots that tried to trip him as he ran. But it wasn't a root that caused him to fall flat on his face – it was something soft and wet, which gave underfoot but offered just enough resistance to send Arthur sprawling.

"Sonofabitch!" Arthur cursed loudly, rubbing his swollen ankle and studying the dead rabbit closely. The blood was only just congealing in its empty eye sockets and it still retained a remnant of body heat. Arthur sighed and pulled himself to his feet, surveying the surrounding woods. The creature couldn't have got far. It was old and almost blind, its muscles surely atrophied by years of confinement. But despite its age and poor physical condition, the beast was still dangerous.

Just then a twig snapped behind Arthur. Startled, the young man cocked his rifle and pointed it in the direction of the sound. Silence. Then a scuffling noise off to the left. Arthur panicked and shot into the bushes. A flurry of wings as a startled bird took off into the evening sky. Arthur's shoulders slumped with relief, but he knew that the evening was far from over. He looked down at the mutilated rabbit and spotted a broken branch nearby; this gave him the clue he needed to ascertain the direction that the creature had taken.

Arthur had been five years old when he first became aware that something was not right in his grandfather's house. Sometimes there were noises at night. Low shuffling sounds, moaning, wailing. Arthur's grandfather had explained that there was a monster in the cellar. Arthur burst into tears and his grandfather comforted him and assured him that the monster could not harm him because it was locked up securely. Arthur asked why grandfather didn't kill it, and the old man explained that it was wrong to kill and that the monster would eventually die on its own. It was grandfather's duty to guard the monster, and one day it would be Arthur's job.

"I don't want to guard the monster!" Arthur shook his head firmly. His grandfather laughed and said not to worry – he would try to live as long as possible to carry out his duty.

Arthur's grandfather had kept his word. He was ninety-three now, and more determined than ever to outlive the creature. But his grandfather was growing progressively more frail, and it was up to Arthur now to feed the creature and see to its basic needs while it still breathed.

Arthur remembered the first time he had seen the beast. It was on his eighth birthday that his grandfather had deemed him old enough to do so. Before unlocking the cellar door, Grandfather gave Arthur a long and boring history lesson about World War II.

"It was a terrible time," he told the boy. "Terrible. Suffering and death everywhere you looked... You never knew what was waiting for you around the corner." Noticing the blank expression in Arthur's eyes, Grandfather decided to get to the point. "Anyway... one day I'd just got back from the east field, and I was going around the side of the barn, when what do you suppose I saw?" The old man's glance at his grandson was rewarded with a yawn, but he was determined to finish his story. "Right there – right in front of me – was a vile monster, a devil from hell itself." Arthur perked up, his eyes widening. "I caught it unawares – it hadn't heard me coming. Well, I wasn't about to wait for it to kill me, so I grabbed the pitchfork that was leaning against the wall and I ran it right through the fuc..." Arthur's eyebrows arched in astonishment, but Grandfather quickly checked himself and carried on, "...the devil. I couldn't kill it because that wouldn't be Christian, but I ran it through right good, then I dragged it here and locked it up, so it could do no more harm."

The last of the light was slowly draining from the sky and Arthur was beginning to feel scared. His swollen ankle was slowing him down, and soon it would be hard to distinguish the trees from the other grey shapes in the forest.

Arthur wondered what havoc the creature could wreak if it remained at large. It must have moved pretty fast to kill the rabbit; Arthur still did not understand how something that old could move so quickly. He wondered if bloodlust – and the creature was not short of that – could have an animating effect. He still had vivid memories of the speed with which the beast had thrown itself at the man from the loan company who had come to take grandfather's telly away. Arthur was thirteen at the time.

"It's in the cellar," Grandfather had told the man.

"Excuse me?"

"The television," Grandfather peered at the man with his cold blue eyes. "It's in the cellar." The man stared at Grandfather uncomprehendingly. "I figured you might be coming for it, so I boxed it up and stored it for you in the cellar."

"I see," the man sounded like he didn't see at all.

"I'd get it for you," continued Grandfather, "but my arthritis has been playing up terribly and my knees make it very hard for me to walk down the steps... I don't suppose you'd mind getting it yourself?" There was a long pause.

"Well..." the man said finally. "Okay."

The man had gone down into the cellar and the creature, which had been dozing in a corner, was upon him in an instant, snarling, biting and tearing. It had all been over in seconds. The other men who came – men from the loan company, developers who wanted to buy grandfather's farm, and even a police officer – had all been dispatched the same way. Some took longer, some took less time, but the creature got them all in the end, and grandfather got to keep his farm and his television set.

Yes, there was no telling how much damage the creature would do if Arthur did not succeed in getting it back to the cellar... or killing it. He could always tell his grandfather that there had been an accident.

Just then, Arthur heard a low feral noise behind him – a kind of hungry growl, full of anticipation and barely-controlled rage. He span round to see the creature crouching by a nearby tree. Arthur's blood froze. He had never seen the creature clearly. It had always been in the half-light of the cellar, and even now it was merging into the shadows of the forest.

Arthur was a little boy again, on his eighth birthday, shaking with fear as his grandfather slowly unlocked the cellar door and let him peer into the darkness.

There was a horrifying, gurgling growl coming from the

corner of the cellar. Then suddenly, a flurry of white, as a thing with a long grey beard and wisps of greasy white hair threw itself towards the stairs where Arthur and his grandfather were standing. Arthur screamed and stumbled back, but his grandfather reassured him.

"Don't worry," he said. "It's on a chain. It can't get to us."

As Arthur watched, the creature reached the bottom of the stairs, yelped and fell, the chain cutting cruelly into its bare ankle. The black tatters of a military uniform hung loosely off its emaciated frame and the silver lightning-like SS signs on the shoulders of the creature's jacket sparkled in the meagre light from the weak light bulb overhead.

Arthur stood in horrified awe – now, as he had then. The creature growled again and started to circle Arthur in the gloom, its milky eyes used to the darkness. Arthur raised his rifle and aimed, but it was too late. The small, rank, drooling creature was upon him, the remains of its rotting teeth already sinking into the soft part of his throat, just under his chin.

Anna Taborska was born in London, England. She is an award-winning filmmaker and writer of horror stories, screenplays and poetry. Anna has directed five films, and worked on seventeen others, with actors such Rutger Hauer, Scott Wilson, Noah Taylor and Jenny Agutter. She was also involved in the making of two major BBC/NBC TV series: Auschwitz: the Nazis and the Final Solution *and* World War Two behind Closed Doors – Stalin, the Nazis and the West. *Anna's stories have appeared in various anthologies, including the* Black Books of Horror *in the UK, and* Best New Writing 2011, Best New Werewolf Tales Vol.1 *and* The Best Horror of the Year Volume Four *in the US. Anna's short story "Bagpuss" was an Eric Hoffer Award Honoree, and the screenplay adaptation of her story "Little Pig" was a finalist in the Shriekfest Film Festival Screenplay Competition, 2009. Anna's debut short story collection,* For Those who Dream Monsters, *is due out in late 2013. You can watch clips from Anna's films (including* The Rain Has Stopped, *winner of two awards at the British Film Festival Los Angeles in 2009) and view her full resume at mdb.com/name/nm1245940.*

PRECIOUS DAMAGED CARGO
by Kerry G. S. Lipp

He giggles as he cocks back and rams his tiny fist into my groin. I don't even see it coming. I double over, not even exaggerating. Tiny fist or not, a shot to the nuts is a shot to the nuts. My nephew got me real good. He's a lot of fun, but all he wants to do is fight. And he likes to punch. And his head is just level with my crotch. You do the math.

"I got you!" he cackles, oblivious to my pain and jumps onto me as I'm keeling over. I swallow the pain and fall like a tackling dummy hit by a line-backer. Now he's raining his tiny fists toward my face. He's still so innocent he can't conceive of inflicting any kind of pain. The nose, like the nuts is a sensitive spot regardless of the size and strength of the fist delivering the blow. But I absolutely love this kid, and I don't get to see him enough so I make the best of it.

I let him go and he backs up down the hall about twenty feet. Comes running at me full bore. Jumps. Tucks. He hits me knees first, curled up into a 4-year-old cannonball. I'm ready this time and defend myself the best I can.

"I'm the good guy. I got you. Good guys always get the bad guys."

"No way. I'm the good guy. I'm Optimus, you're Starscream," I say this knowing full well what the reaction is going to be. I'm never going to physically retaliate on the boy, despite the pain he's put me through in the last few minutes, but I'm sure as hell not above taunting him.

"Transform!" I shout and sit up, making robot noises. He's not having it.

"Umm Uncle Shane," he starts, pauses, gets his words together. "Umm Uncle Shane, I'm always the good guy, you're Starscream okay?"

"No way STARSCREAM," I come at him and pick him up, still making robot sounds. He screams, horrified, as I lift him over my head, a professional wrestler manhandling a midget. Wailing, he flings his arms and legs but none of them connect.

"I'm sorry Starscream, but I must end you," I say in my best Optimus voice. He's sobbing now, little innocent tears slowly leaking down his puffed up tomato face.

Is it wrong that this is somewhat satisfying? Taunting a 4 year old? I don't think so.

Raising him even higher, I body slam him into the couch, dropping him 3 or 4 feet. He bounces, looks at me, and mad as he is, he can't hide his delight. The boy loves to fight. The delight is only there for a split-second.

"Once again the earth is safe from that pest, Starscream! The good guys win!" I say, looking right at him.

The delight falls from his face and his smile twists into the defeated disgust only visible on the face of a toddler.

"Grandpa," he yells and takes off running. Grandpa doesn't even have a chance to answer. Tiny fists are knocking on his thighs. Junior is rapping on them. Not fighting fists like he does with me, instead, knocking like Grandpa's legs are twin doors. Grandpa has been witnessing the whole exchange with something akin to amused horror.

"What chu want boy? Uncle Shane picking on you? Want me to get him?"

"Um. Grandpa. Uncle Shane said that I'm Starscream and he is Optimus, but Grandpa, I'm the good guy. The good guys win. I get to be Optimus. I'm Optimus right Grandpa?"

"I think you make a really good Starscream," I fire at the little boy. He shrieks. Tears again. Tugging at Grandpa, looking for anything.

Grandpa shoots me an "I'm not dealing with this anymore look." One I've seen before that means, "One more taunt and you're on your own."

"Should we get him Optimus?" Grandpa asks, picking Junior up. "We'll teach him who the good guys are."

"Yeah! Let's get him, we're the good guys. Right Grandpa?"

"Right."

Grandpa, who is my father, gives me another look. I get it. I've got to become the bad guy and let the good guys win. While taunting Junior is a lot of fun, taking it too far for too long is

148

something my heart wasn't built for. Sometimes just the sight of this little boy being an innocent little boy is enough to twist my guts in the most beautiful of ways. Something about him never being backhanded by the world is painfully poetic. Something you can only see in little kids, amplified to an extreme if it's one that's close to you. I'm jealous of him. But not because of the attention he gets or anything like that. I'm jealous of his never-ending inquisitive ambition, his innocence and his clean slate. Looking at Junior, who probably isn't a whole lot different from how I was at four, makes me wonder just what the fuck happens to people. It seems like the older we get the more we lose. I suppose it's only fitting then that Junior is the good guy and I'm the bad guy.

They rush at me, Grandpa holding the little booger out like he's got Iron Man on a leash. Crashing down on me, Junior is all giggles, anger and sadness forgotten as we wrestle and I let him win. Children amaze me; anger and sadness snap to delight like a switch, grudges drop and all is taken fresh. They live completely in the moment.

Grandpa acts like a referee and does a quick three count, and raises Junior's hand high above his head.

"We got him didn't we?" Junior asks, high-fiving Grandpa. "We're the good guys aren't we?"

I roll and groan on the floor. "You got me good Optimus. I'm scared of you!"

He comes over and helps me up as much as his little body will allow. Both his little hands tug on my wrist. "Um. Next time you can be a good guy with me Uncle Shane." This is one of those moments that break your heart in the sweetest of ways.

"Deal."

"Who wants a snack?" Grandpa asks, and starts walking towards the kitchen.

"I do," Junior shouts and takes off running ahead of him. Then he stops, turns and runs back to me. He wraps his small hand around my index finger and we walk together. My heart breaks in that sweet way all over again.

"Plans have changed," Grandpa, my dad, says to me. "Can you take him back for us?"

149

"Are you serious?" I'm great with the boy, but I've never spent more than a couple hours alone with him and now I'm responsible for driving him four hours back to his mom? It's not that I'm untrustworthy, but it's a bit surprising all the same.

"We can't drive him back tomorrow, so we were hoping you could drop him on your way back this tonight."

"This is ok with Becky?" Becky is Junior's mother and my brother's ex-girlfriend. She's cool and she likes me but still.

"Why wouldn't it be?"

"I don't know, she's just so protective of him and I've never even babysat him for very long, let alone driving with him in my car. I mean it's fine with me, but you're all ok with it?"

He looks at me like I've lost my mind. "Uh yeah Shane," he says, "it's fine. You're good with him, he adores you. You're his Uncle; this will be a great opportunity to bond."

I look at the table where Junior is eating a snack. He's eating bananas with a dollop of peanut butter and topped with a chocolate chip. I remember holding him in my arms for the first time, feeding him a bottle. I'm blown away at the way he's grown, aged, and retained his innocence. I have no kids of my own, but I'm so attached to this little boy, that I'm starting to appreciate the way in which a child drastically changes the course of life of the parents.

He holds out a banana slice and I chomp it from his fingers. My father is right, this will be an excellent bonding experience. I think of my relationship with my favourite uncle. Of everything he's done for me. Spanning from childhood well into adulthood, times he helped me, secrets that we have, trips he's taken me on and that barely scratches the surface. Shit, he's cleaned up my messes more times than you can count on one hand and never judged me for a one. Never lectured me and never told on me. Omerta. He just took care of me and kept it a secret because that's what an uncle does.

I realize that I've been a good uncle, but I want to be a great one, and that this is a chance to develop a milestone on that path.

"OK," I say. "I'm OK with that, but I've never done anything like this before, what do I need to know?"

"Just treat him like an intelligent pet," my father says. The thing about my dad is that he never, ever, laughs at his own jokes, so sometimes he's hard to read. I don't think he's kidding, and he's not. Honestly, what is a toddler but an intelligent, sometimes confrontational pet? They are loyal because they have to be and they know that you are their master, and even when difficult, in the end, they will mind you.

"We'll put the car seat in your car and strap the DVD player to the seat in front of him and he'll probably be either into the show or taking a nap the whole time. But even with him watching or sleeping, this is a great opportunity to be his protector and develop a stronger bond. You need to do this Shane. Trust your instincts. Just don't do anything stupid, and you'll be fine."

I can't really argue with his logic.

"So if I stop at a gas station and go inside do I have to take him in with me?"

"Trust your instincts," my father tells me. "It's not raging hot out, so if he's asleep and you go in, park close, and watch him like a hawk. If he's awake, take him inside, get him a treat, and use him as a prop to open a conversation with a cute blonde."

We both laugh and I feel a little better.

"Anything I need to worry about that I'm too naïve to see in advance?" I ask.

"Quit being so goddamn hard on yourself. Your piss-poor confidence is pissing me off."

Ouch.

"The only thing you need to worry about is that he knows how to let himself out of his car seat. He knows he's not supposed to, but it's still something he can do. If he does, pull over, strap him back in and threaten to give him a time out if he does it again. That should be enough. And make sure the child safety switch on your back door is flipped up. We don't want him rolling down the highway."

I laugh. He doesn't laugh. Another dad comment.

"OK, I can handle that. And if I need anything you and mom both keep your phones on. OK?"

"Of course we will! You are twenty-five years old for God's sake," my dad says. "You've got nothing to worry about Shane. Just take care of that precious cargo."

"Yeah! You can do it uncle Shane!" the parrot chirps from the peanut gallery. They are both right. This will be a great bonding experience and I am more than capable. I consider the absolute worst case scenarios, and I reaffirm to myself that at the very least, I can keep this little boy alive.

"Arms," I say and he lifts his arms, I slip them through the straps and lock him in.

"We're both good guys aren't we?" he asks.

"Right now we are," I say as I slide the arm belts into the slot between his legs. I hate doing this. I always feel like I'm going to smash his balls, but he doesn't seem to notice.

"Here," I say and hand him two of his action figures. The two that I grab blind out of the bag are Optimus and Starscream, I suppose it's only fitting.

"Um Uncle Shane? Can I have one more good guy. I'm Optimus but you can be the other good guy?"

I smile to myself and reach back into the bag and fish out another good guy Transformer. The name of the new one is Bumblebee. I hand it to him.

"Give Grandpa a hug and then we can go see mommy," I say.

I'm really bad at goodbyes and this is when I can feel pressure on the dam. I duck out and my father leans in. Watching my parents interact with my brother's little boy is almost surreal. I can't really put it into words. The best that I can do is say that it really makes me appreciate everything that I've ever experienced. I know that that is extreme and vague, but it's the truth. It's like witnessing pure love on pure steroids.

And now I'm supposed to be an integral part of all of this. Taking Junior on this trip is like being the guy on the bench offered his chance to contribute on the quest for a championship. Even if that guy is full of doubts, his teammates and his coach are full of confidence and encouragement and he has no choice but to step up. The only thing worse than failure is refusing to try. This is why we're all here after all, isn't it? Throw me the ball. I can take care of this little boy.

Stepping back and watching Junior and Grandpa say goodbye, I feel the unwelcome sting of tears. I fight them off. They hug, share goodbyes. As Grandpa closes the door, Junior says one last time, "Bye bye grandpa, I love you." If this doesn't melt your fucking heart, kill yourself.

Me and my father do an awkward man hug that we still can't

quite seem to get right which is funny to me considering the perfect hug he just gave Junior with about twenty-one years less experience. He tells me to call him if I need anything.

As I'm backing out of the driveway, my father knocks on my window. I suck at goodbyes and he's the kind of guy that needs to say it at least three times. I roll it down. He looks me in the eye, "You're going to be fine," he says. "Trust your gut, do the right things and take care of the precious cargo."

I fight the tears, half from the goodbye, half from the proud, confident moment I'm having with my dad. "Will do," I say. "I'll call you if I need anything and I'll definitely call you when I drop him off with Becky."

"Bye bye Grandpa!" Junior chirps from the back seat.

My father smiles, pats of the top of the car, and I raise the window. Me and Junior wave goodbye at my father waving goodbye at us.

All of us equally unaware that we never checked the child safety lock on the door in the back seat.

I'd never driven with someone in the back seat and no one riding shotgun before. It's kind of weird. Equally weird is watching a toddler that isn't yours. It's like being hypnotized. I think that when you're not used to dealing with one, their behaviour is a lot more hypnotic, but when they belong to you and you must witness said behaviour on a constant basis it loses its power. Not being used to his behaviour, I am intrigued by the two-on-one war raging in the back seat.

"Who's winning back there?" I ask. The smack of plastic on plastic and mouth sound effects stops for a second.

"Optimus," he says. "The good guys always win. We're the good guys aren't we Uncle Shane?"

"We sure are," I answer, happy at how content he is. My dad was right, this was going to be easy. All I had to do was keep the car between the lines. Building the bond was easy too. I was protecting him, he may not consciously remember later, but subconsciously he would. I smile, considering this first milestone, me on my way to being a great person in the eyes of this young life.

Two hours into the trip I do something stupid. Junior was

asleep by then and I thought I could get away with it. I had been at my parent's house for 2 days. That meant 2 days without a cigarette. They don't know I smoke and I don't want them to know. I survived the weekend and almost the road trip, but when I glance in the mirror and see Junior sleeping, a temporary Transformer truce; the Camels started talking to me.

I did it.

As I lit the cigarette the idea of innocence and the difference between me and Junior and my parents and Junior and Junior and the world set my brain on fire. I couldn't really make any cogent connections, but there is definitely something to it. If anyone knew what I was doing right now, and even though I knew a couple of them smoked, they probably would've killed me.

I stop at a red light, and Junior utters something between a whimper and a cough as I watch him in the rear-view through the smoky haze. This kid has an effect on me. Once again his innocence hits me like a sledgehammer to the tailbone. I look at my Camel. I look at Junior. I look at myself in the mirror. All of these images clouded through the billowing, cancerous smoke. I make a decision. He coughs again, harder this time. I take another glance at the road; the light is still red, it says stop. I look at my cigarette. The cherry is red, it says stop. I look in the mirror again, Junior's face is turning red, it says stop. I hit it one more time before I stop.

My window is cracked a couple inches and I put it down all the way. I look at the cigarette tucked between my index and middle finger on my left hand. I pinch it, thumb and index finger, make a deal with myself. This is the last hit. I close my eyes, inhale deep, hold it, hold it, and blow it out slow. Open my eyes, stare myself down in the mirror and pitch the cigarette out as far and as hard as I can. I'm done with that shit. I already feel better.

The still burning half-cigarette hits a guy on a motorcycle next to me at the light right in the face. The red ashes spray like fireflies. He turns and looks at me, hairy arm muscles flexing in his leather vest, face turning as red at the stoplight. He bats a muscled arm at his own face, looks at me, and jumps off his bike.

There is a line of cars behind me and a stream of cars passing through the intersection. There is literally nowhere for me to go. This is not good. He's off his bike and heading toward me.

I've got about six seconds. I can't go anywhere. It surprises even me, when my first instinct in this situation is to protect Junior instead of myself, but it's the truth. I really don't care what happens, as long as the boy is untouched. The only way to salvage whatever is left of my soul is to protect the innocence of this little boy. I roll my window up as fast as I can. The pressure from my finger is hard enough to snap the switch.

"What the fuck man?" the biker shouts as he strides toward my car, leaving his bike idling in the lane next to me.

He can't hear what I'm saying through the window of the car, but I can hear him. I'm really scared, but more than that, I'm scared that Junior is going to wake up. Wake up and be scarred for life.

The biker knocks twice on my window, and I can hear his bike running behind him. "Get out of the fucking car," he shouts, face all in my window and I can see the burn-mark on his face where my cigarette hit him.

As I'm reaching for the button to lower the window, he puts his fist through it. There is nothing on earth like the sound of glass shattering, especially when it is the only thing protecting you from the enemy. Shit is about to get real ugly. My last action before the inevitable escalation of violence is to turn my head and look into the back seat. Junior is somehow still sleeping. When I look back through the broken window at the biker, I can see that he is looking at the boy in the back seat.

He reaches in with both hands and grabs my collar. "I don't know what's worse, you piece of shit," he says. "You hitting me in the face with that butt or you blowing that shit into this little boy's face. How fucking dumb are you?"

I can't really argue with him. I'm about to deserve whatever I get, but no matter how much we deserve our punishment, we still have an instinct to survive. I suppose it's the lizard brain.

Regardless, I had one choice, and that was to get out of this, and not let Junior know a thing about it. Never mind that he'd tell the story of what happened, but he couldn't witness this. The easy job was transporting him, the hard job was doing it without threatening his innocence. I'm not trying to be dramatic here but this is a big deal. Everybody trusted me, and here I am trading words at this intersection with a biker twice my size. And it's my fault.

The biker's hands jump from my collar to my throat and I

can feel my face turning red, as if telling my breath to stop. "How can you blow that shit in that little boy's face?" he shouts and pulls me through the shattered driver's side window.

"Stop it. Please," I mutter as I land hard on the pavement. Pain blows like bolts up and down my legs. Car headlights from behind us illuminate the scene. No one comes to investigate, they are all simply watching.

"How can you blow that shit in that little boy's face?" he screams again and kicks me in the face.

I feel my nose snap and a tooth or two shake loose. Blood is pouring out of my face like thick red water from a flesh cup. He's got steel toes on. The blood is red, forming a small circle under my face on the blacktop. The biker doesn't stop. He kicks me in the side. Snap.

"I'm sorry. I'm sorry. Stop. I quit. Please," I beg him. And it's the truth, double meaning intended. I want nothing more to do with cigarettes or the beating that I'm taking. Can't he see the red? It means stop.

When he kicks me in the face again I realize that he means to kill me. And no one is going to come to my aid.

And then from the car I hear, "Get him Uncle Shane!"

At this point I'm so fucked up I don't know what to think. I don't think anything, but with him yelling like that, I KNOW I don't give up. I scramble around on the ground, dodging as many kicks as I take.

When you beg for mercy, and mercy isn't granted, the only thing left to do is fight back. The biker lands another kick and I flop over. I open my eyes. Lying next to my face is the biggest, most hateful shard of glass I've ever seen. Knowing how bad it would slice my hand open and not caring I squeeze my fist around it. I feel it cut, and that pain feels like hope.

As the biker pulls his foot back for another kick I dodge and roll and slice at his Achilles tendon with the jagged shard of glass in my fist. Blood shoots from the wound like a bottle uncorked and I hear a sound like a wound rope unravelling. I think I actually see the severed tendon shoot up his leg like a worm on fire. He shrieks and falls to his knees. I think I hear a car door. We are surrounded and my mind is torn between being shocked that it takes this long for someone to come and being shocked that someone would even come at all. Me and the biker are both on our knees, battered, staring at each other and he swings a desperate punch that glances off the side of my head.

Somebody stop this.

Nobody does. He swings again.

I look in his eyes, and see no calculation, only desperation, he is like a cornered and wounded tiger, flailing and clawing and lethal. He dives at me hands once again encircling my neck. There is red everywhere, but we don't stop.

Something between a gnarled grimace and a sinister smile cuts his mouth as he shoots murder at me with his eyes. Realizing that he is going to kill me, whoever had gotten out of the car wasn't stopping him, and that I still had the glass shard in my hand, I close my eyes and play dead.

After a few moments, he relaxes and I stab him in the side of the neck. Our blood mixes. We are both covered in it. His hands go from my neck to his own. Bright red blood bubbles through his fingers and drips into my eyes. I see everything through a film of red as he falls on his back. I have to finish him. Blind with rage and drunk on bloodlust I fall on top of him and then I feel a small poke on my shoulder and hear a tiny voice.

I look and see Junior and he is red. To this day I'm not sure if he was already covered in blood or if I just saw him that way, but I hand him a glass shard. He takes it and pokes the biker softly below his eye. A small trickle of blood rolls down the biker's cheek.

"I got him," Junior gushes with glee and jabs him again.

Together we stab the biker until his heart stops and his eyes glaze over and when the hot tears finally flush the bloody red rage from my eyes, I get a clear look at the scene. Junior is still stabbing the biker with the shard of glass, not even knowing that his own tiny hand is cut, let alone the damage his hand had dealt. My nephew is covered in blood. Red means stop I think, standing up.

"That's enough," I say. "Come here."

Dropping the glass, he giggles and runs to me, blood covered arms wrapping around my left leg.

"We got him didn't we Uncle Shane? We got him because we're the good guys! He was a bad guy wasn't he?"

"He was something," I say.

What have I done?

I fall to my knees, holding my arms out and looking Junior in his innocent, blood-drenched eyes, the lights of an approaching siren flashing red on his little face. The red means stop, and I pray that this is the end of it.

And then the stoplight turns green.

Kerry G.S. Lipp *is a wannabe writer, working hard to drop the wannabe part. He teaches English at a community college by evening and writes horrible things by night. He hates the sun. His parents recently started reading his stories and it appears that he is now out of the will. Kerry's work will be featured in several anthologies in 2013 including* War Is Hell *from Cruentus Libri Press and* DOA 2 *from Blood Bound Books. KGSL blogs weekly about writing at www.HorrorTree.com and maintains his own website www.newworldhorror.com. He's also constantly working on new short stories and a novel. Say hi on Twitter @kerrylipp or check out his Facebook author page: New World Horror – Kerry G.S. Lipp.*

MOTHER
by Keith Brooke

"Mother's dead." Tilana's voice was strong. Her words numbed me but deep within I felt the anticipation, the realisation that change was due. I blocked it out.

Thorn and jent had been arguing when Tilana appeared. We were in a small clearing on the oakwood slopes, nearly two hours from the village; we had been digging combe-roots for most of the morning, hacking away at their tough skins to let the sweet juices solidify, then sacking them for transportation and storage.

I was waist-deep in the pit, tugging at a difficult corm, when I sensed the atmosphere growing tight. Over the buzz of the grade-flies I heard thorn say that he had been taken into the Core again. "What a chore," he said. "You'd think they'd give a man a break." He laughed. I knew the taunting tone in his voice. Jent had probably provoked him but thorn was always too ready to retaliate.

The three of us are of much the same age but the Women of our village have clearly taken a special liking to thorn. They have called him six times, if his stories are the truth. I have no reason to doubt him. He is young, fast, healthy. He has a charm apparent to us all. But he also knows how to choose his targets. He can boast to me all he likes and I'll grin and take it, I don't resent his good fortune. I am bound to be called at some date or another: the Women know the value of diversity. But jent will never be called. He was born with his left forearm absent, the hand joined at a precarious angle to the elbow. Such deformity is a frequent occurrence, affecting many more Females than males. Jent will never receive his summons to the Core: no Woman would take such a risk.

"Hey, thorn, will you give me some help?" I am accustomed to breaking up the fights of my two friends. They are close, as the songs say we should be, but there has always been a tension between them. I smeared a muddy hand across my forehead and glared, my hands on my hips, a Woman's pose, when She is mediator. Thorn grinned nonchalantly and slid a cut combe-root into his sack but jent took a step towards him, spat at his feet.

That was when I spotted Tilana. Tilana is my blood sister: from womb to puberty we were closer than brothers but now she is Woman, now she is Nameless. Tilana is no more.

We are not supposed to distinguish between the Nameless — they are Woman — but Tilana has always retained her individuality for me. Self-consciously, I rubbed the mud from my forehead.

Just then, the sight of Woman made me defensive. They shouldn't come out this far, not alone: the Women of our village are too few, we cannot afford to lose any to the dangers of the forest. She was breaking the codes.

When Tilana's eyes fixed on us I wondered if it was she who had called thorn into the Core. He probably wouldn't know: to him there are no distinctions.

She headed towards us and I scrambled out of my combe pit and pushed between jent and thorn for a sack. "Come on," I muttered, "you're getting behind." I hacked at a root and slid it into the bag and was relieved when thorn and then jent resumed their work. Most men do not object when one of the Nameless intervenes in a dispute, but my signal was obvious. Thorn and jent are my friends — there was nothing serious enough to warrant interference — and Tilana was my sister. We did not need her judgment.

But she was still approaching so I looked up again. Tilana is tall and strong, her skin dark and smooth. I often wonder why she has never called me to the Core. I am healthy, surely I deserve such an opportunity? I wondered why she should approach us out there in the oakwoods and then I sensed that something was wrong.

"Mother's dead," she said. That was all, and now she has left us again, with our combe-roots and our thoughts.

Mother is the voice of the gods. She is our channel to the heavens. Also She governs the village, She guides the Nameless, directs the course of their lives. As Woman is to man, so Mother is to Woman. Now our village is without a Mother and the world is a darker place.

We must be cautious if we are to survive the four days until the moon is full and we have a new Mother. We are lucky. In the past there has been longer to wait. For these four days the Women of the village will not leave the central circle of huts we call the Core;

160

so we, the men, are unprotected, unguided in this hostile world. There are perhaps ten dozen of us, cowering in our huts that cluster around the Core, but without our seventeen precious Women we are emasculate. The order of our lives has vanished. It is an exciting time, a nervous time, tensions are close to the surface. Things will be better when we have a new Mother.

It is cold out here, on the edge of the village. We can light no fires without a Mother to shield us from the gods. Our food is uncooked and goes largely uneaten: our emotions interfere with the traditional patterns. After a time, the sounds of argument merge into the background. It is three days since Mother died and, without mediation, our aggression is always ready to erupt. I have experienced such times twice in my adult life but on both occasions I was too young to understand. Now I can see it all about, I can feel it in my spleen. We fight because we are without guidance, we fight because the Woman in us all is hidden deep within; but more, we fight because we are scared. The continuity of our existence has been fractured, we are lost.

I breathe deeply. So far I have avoided the petty squabbles and conflicts. By tomorrow night we will have a new Mother — I shudder at the thought: the anticipation breaks all barriers — and then life will settle again.

Glancing towards the Core I spot something, a figure edging through the shadows. Curious, I follow. Quickly I recognise the confident movements of thorn, even as he clings to darkness.

I hurry after him. "Thorn," I whisper. It is the first time I have spoken since Tilana told us the news. I have kept my distance, these three days. Closeness merely breeds conflict at such times.

He is frightened. He jerks at the sound of my voice, turns sharply. I see his eyes narrow in the light of the nearly full moon. "You," he says dismissively, and in that instant I realise that my isolation has only been partly due to my own efforts: perhaps sensing my mood, my friends have been avoiding me. Then he shrugs and turns. "Come on," he says. "I want to see what's happening."

He is going to spy, he is going to break the codes in order to alleviate his own share of the tension we all feel. What can I do? I can leave him, pretend to myself that I have not seen him this night, fight alone with my conscience. I can raise the alarm and so prevent his transgression, but by so doing I might implicate myself and my current mood is one of tense caution. Or I can go with him, try to modify his actions, guide him with my own restraint.

I follow him through the moon-cast shadows of the huts. These inner huts in the men's cluster are used for storage, roots and juice and nuts and grains, tools and firewood and winter clothing. There is an open space between these huts and the Core, a space kept clear of vegetation. Thorn wants to cross this space but I catch his arm and lead him around to the south side where there is a rocky outcrop that extends halfway towards the Core. We reach the innermost boulder and I say, "No farther, thorn: the codes."

He shrugs, relieved, I think, that I am here to curb his impetuosity.

There is a convenient gap between the Women's huts, where the long bulk of the crèche disrupts the regular pattern. The children should be asleep now, but I know from experience that the tension reaches into the crèche too. From our uncomfortable viewpoint we can see right through the circle of huts and into the heart of our village.

The Women are gathered in their debating circle but my eyes are drawn first to Mother, nailed to Her cross, Her head tilted up, pale in the light of the moon. Stripped of Her robes, Her body is horribly thin and wasted. Her face is like a skull, Her ribs stand free, Her... I tear my eyes away. She has been our Mother for four years, a long time in the service of the gods. Tomorrow, the Women will heap wood around the cross and the new Mother will light the first fire of Her reign. It will be a wonderful event.

A safe distance from the cross is the joss-house and in it, the throne that Mother must only ever leave when the moon is full and the flow is to be praised.

Thorn is restless, his plans defused, only half-realised. From our outcrop we can see everything but the voices from the debating circle only reach us as a half-heard murmur, the words indistinct, susurrating.

"*Who do you think will be chosen?*" says thorn, breaking the codes again. Speculation is the seed of the night, something to which we are vulnerable when we are left unprotected, as now. I touch the rock. Contact with the Earth is always a comfort.

In the past it is said that Mother was always one who had bred, one who had proven Her fruitfulness. In my time She has always been chosen from the fresh, the unproven. The codes say our Mother must never bear children. It is the way.

I sit until the sky begins to lighten and then I leave, realising that boredom must have taken thorn long before.

At some time in the night I recognised the figure that had been holding the circle rapt. One Woman distinct from the others. Tilana. It was then that this nervous anticipation took form in my mind. I looked for a long time at the animated figure of my sister, the shadows she cast, and then I felt the fear and, more than anything, the joy. As I return to the hut I share with jent and thorn I keep reminding myself that it is mere supposition, I have no way of knowing. Not until tonight.

The night is sharp like a blade. Alone, I can taste the frost on the still air. The stars burn more brightly than I have ever known. Atmosphere is a powerful drug.

We are already gathered by the firewood hut when the horn blows, drawn together by some subconscious magnetism. Here, the taste of frost is absent, the warm fug of bodies smothering all else. We are men together.

So I tell myself. It has a reassuring shape in my mind, such a thought. The tension is greater than ever but there is no arguing, no aggression. Tonight is the night of the full moon, the Bleeding Moon, as the Women call it and the men are not supposed to know.

The horn, the horn. A single, plaintive note, not loud but heard by us all. We stir, this crowd of men, and then we process solemnly past the storage huts, heading towards the Core.

It feels wrong to be walking openly across this space, the barrier between male and Female, but we proceed regardless. Most of the men are older than me; I guess that more than half — maybe as many as seventy — have made this journey alone, heading for a night of service to the tribe. Maybe that is why it feels wrong: copulation is a private thing, yet now we cross the boundary en masse, called by the horn and the full, Bleeding Moon.

During the day the Women formed a chain between firewood

hut and Core, passing kindling, branches, logs, from hand to hand, Woman to Woman. The children helped, too, but now they will be locked inside their crèche. They will pay their respects to Mother tomorrow.

Our tight-nerved procession passes through the circle formed by the Women's huts, the outer perimeter of the Core. We stare at the ground, watch the placing of our feet, but in the periphery I can see the huge pyre they have built around our dead Mother. She is still staring at the moon.

The Women stand in a circle around the unlit fire, heads turned downwards. The scene is lit by the stars and the moon. I stare at the ground.

We spread ourselves out until we form a wide circle that encloses the Women and the waiting fire. We look up, finally, and I see that Mother's throne has been moved from the joss-house so that it now stands to one side of the huge pyre.

The Women start to hum and then they turn to face outwards and we join in. We have to sing to the elements, you see. We must follow the codes if our Mother is to be effective in protecting us from the world. Earth, Fire, Soul, Water, Air, Flesh.

The songs lift us. I can almost forget what is happening. Beside me, thorn, and on the other side, jent, sing our hymn, one strong and loud, the other weak and barely audible. As ever, I am between them. I sing with spirit but I do not have a voice like thorn's.

After a full song-cycle the Women stop singing but they are so few that the volume of our chorus barely drops. They go down to their knees, press their lips to the soil. One of them holds a bronze pot aloft and chants the secret Female names of the elements three times over. Then She tips the pot and pours its dark red contents into the soil. It is said that this is part of a monthly ceremony but a man cannot know for sure. I watch and sing as the blood pools on the soil and its steam rises. It will be soon now: we will have a Mother again. Thorn's voice comes to my mind: Who do you think will be chosen? Now is a legitimate time to think such thoughts. Now the moment is near.

I study the Women, each an individual, yet they are the Nameless, indistinguishable. Surely the time must be close!

Then one of the Women steps into a space, raises Her hands to the Bleeding Moon, tips Her head back. I recognise those rapt features and suddenly I am scared, no, ecstatic... I cannot keep up with the flickering state of my emotions and so I stop trying. All I can do is try to appear calm. I must not spoil things now.

I watch as Tilana — my sister, how I desperately want to think of her as such! — kneels and traces a finger through the pooled blood of the village's women. Then her entire hand, spreading the dark stain, seizes a fistful of the bloodied soil.

When she stands and turns I know it is true, I know that it is meant to be.

I appear to have lost some time because suddenly she is before me. She reaches out, smears the blood and soil over my forehead and along each of my cheekbones.

I feel alone and scared and overjoyed. The men around me have rearranged themselves, isolating me in their envy and their awe.

I am overcome, I lose more time, look around, recognise where I am. They have carried me across and placed me in the Mother throne; now I am truly at the Core.

Now it is the women who are singing alone, a low, apparently tuneless hymn, a secret anthem that I know I must have heard before and still cannot remember. The women are around me and I forget the men, that is all gone. Even my fear has gone by now.

I am serene as I stretch and look up at Tilana, at the blade she is holding. A faint, physical tug and one of the women has removed my cloth.

As the blade touches my skin and Tilana sets about parting me from my manhood I know that physical pain has become a constant part of my life — however long that may be, before the fevers or the Great Weakness take hold — and that the pain will peak each month as my wounds are reopened under the Bleeding Moon, but that no longer concerns me.

I look down. Tilana's task is done, let the red flow be praised. Our village has a new Mother. It is the way.

Keith Brooke's first novel, Keepers of the Peace, *appeared in 1990, since when he has published seven more adult novels, six collections, and over 70 short stories. For ten years from 1997 he ran the web-based SF, fantasy and horror showcase* infinity plus *(www.infinityplus.*

165

co.uk), *featuring the work of around 100 top genre authors, including Michael Moorcock, Stephen Baxter, Connie Willis, Gene Wolfe, Vonda McIntyre and Jack Vance.* Infinity plus *has recently been relaunched as an independent publishing imprint producing print and ebooks. His novel* Genetopia *was published by Pyr in February 2006 and was their first title to receive a starred review in Publishers Weekly;* The Accord, *published by Solaris in 2009, received another starred PW review and was optioned for film. His most recent novel,* Harmony *(published in the UK as* alt.human*), is a big exploration of aliens, alternate history and the Fermi paradox published in 2012 by Solaris, and shortlisted for the Philip K Dick Award. 2012 also saw publication of* Strange Divisions and Alien Territories: the Sub-genres of Science Fiction, *an academic exploration of SF from the perspectives of a dozen top authors in the field (edited by Keith Brooke, published by Palgrave Macmillan). Writing as Nick Gifford, his teen fiction is published by Puffin, with one novel also optioned for the movies by Andy Serkis and Jonathan Cavendish's Caveman Films. He writes reviews for The Guardian, teaches creative writing at the University of Essex, and lives with his wife Debbie in Wivenhoe, Essex.*

DOWNSIZE
by Allen Ashley

My first time in the loyalty chair was characterised by a sudden sharp pain gradually followed by dreaming bliss. This was essentially how I imagined the injection of a Class A drug might feel. I had no personal experience to draw on, however, and, indeed, suffer from a generalised aversion to needles.

The vision lasted for about fifteen minutes in real time though my somnolent mind perceived a much longer duration. I was transported back to a recollection of younger years: fairly accurate but *mended*, rose-tinted and golden rather than grey, dreary and urban. I was a little loath to leave this better version behind.

I felt hardly changed afterwards, although I undoubtedly was. Maybe the effect would be stronger in the cumulative rather than the singular. With the way the global economy was shrinking, I felt sure I'd have another turn in the loyalty chair again quite soon.

The gents' toilet of Hirojima Financial was, as usual, a repository of rumours.

"I heard there's restructuring going on. Serious downsizing."

"Can't be worse than Jones And Co. They sacked all the cleaners there last month so everybody left has to get in half an hour earlier every day to hoover the floors and shine the taps and stuff. *And* they have to take the hand towels home and launder them."

"That's nothing. The DG's secretary at Platt Systems has had to start going down on him twice a week just to stay on the payroll!"

"You're having me on!"

"No, I'm not. Good job she's not a bloke, I s'pose."

"Who told you this?"

"Just the old fashioned grapevine, mate. No smoke without fire, if you know what I mean. Anyway, gotta get back to my desk. Don't want to be in the firing line."

I washed my own hands quickly and held them under the

foetid hot air drier till I could see no more coagulating drops. I walked rather than use the lift. Got to get some sort of exercise apart from RSI and eye strain. At the far wall of the department the dollar sign glowed large and red, the lower case e representing the Euro remained strong and white but the blue pound sign seemed fainter, smaller. The fluctuating market had changed even during my brief nature call. Sometimes matters moved with remarkable haste, other times the illuminations glowed with constant static precision for days and nights on end.

On the way back to my screen, I passed the lovely Christine, who continued to resist my polite but definite amorous overtures. She was wearing a short-sleeved white blouse and her downy arms moved over the keyboard with the grace of a pianist. She threw back her bobbed blonde hair but ignored me as I passed. Steve was at my desk, cribbing some export figures for the last quarter.

"Have you heard?" I began.

"Yeah. Big time downsizing. We'll be all right, though, mate. You been in that loyalty chair yet?"

"Just the once. You?"

He unbuttoned his cuff and showed me his small blue implant. "Any day now, I hope," he smiled. "I tell you what, Dave, I think me and you'll be OK. I reckon we've got jobs here for life if we want them."

That's a big if, I thought but didn't say.

Beyond the window, the staff of Salt Mine Securities buzzed as busily as ever and in the street below the shoppers and skiving commuters crawled like worker ants. Life as normal.

In the constant shadow of the sword of Damocles.

The Divisional Chairman, Mr St John, called a general staff meeting at six-thirty on Friday. I could see that several of my colleagues were itching to let off steam down the pub or catch commuter trains back to long-suffering families but aside from a few stifled yawns, nobody let on at the inconvenience of the forced, unpaid overtime.

"I just wanted to reassure all of you that we are maintaining a continued commitment to our current workforce," he began. "Yes, you will undoubtedly experience some hardship during this period of shrinkage but, as I'm sure you're aware, in the current climate we must look at and indeed *grasp* every opportunity to cut our costs. I believe we will be able to emerge from this with a slimmed-down but more efficient and indeed *healthier* workforce. Any questions?"

Caroline cleared her throat and nervously asked, "Are you saying in effect that everyone is going to be forced to undergo the ordeal of the loyalty chair?"

"Well, I wouldn't exactly describe it as an ordeal, my dear."

"I've heard it will interfere with my ability to bear children."

"The old conundrum, I'm afraid: family or career. But to answer your question, it's likely that we may make further use of the loyalty chair. With suitable modifications. It's really nothing to be afraid of," he smiled.

The pregnant silence was only punctuated by an embarrassed rustling of papers and slight shuffling of feet.

"Well, if there's no further questions... Good. I trust you will all have an enjoyable and relaxing weekend."

I went home on one of those new tube trains which has extra standing room and, surprisingly enough, a higher ceiling. Not that the tunnels are any different. No, I'm not sure how they work that out, either. I managed not to think about work too much and on the Saturday I was down at the Emirates trying to see past the tall bloke in front of me as we struggled to trounce Rickman Forest one nil. We didn't look that convincing but so what because we simply serenaded their supporters with "Going down, going down, going down!" for the best part of the ninety minutes. They really are doomed and good riddance. Their fans were cunts when we went up to their place. Like the nineteen eighties all over again.

By Sunday, however, my daydreams and attempted morning lie-in were full of fiscal illuminations. If you stared at the markers long enough during a slack period you started to see all sorts of things as the rods and cones burned out in your overloaded irises. The modern equivalent of the cave or camp fire, I suppose. I caught the train back to the office, stared up at the huge building so rightly, if quaintly, described as a skyscraper. I felt dwarfed by a physical artefact and a global concept so much greater than I. The front door was firmly locked and security turned me away from the side entrance. I tried to explain that I only wanted to go in and do a little work in order to be one step ahead of the game on Monday, but nothing doing.

Walking back from the station I got caught in a sudden downpour. The specially treated fibres of my suit were supposed to be shrink-proof but you never knew and I had to dig my spare one out from the back of the wardrobe, still polythene wrapped from the dry cleaners and just a little loose on the shoulders.

Caroline's desk had been cleared by eight-thirty on Monday.

"Salt Mine are trying to beat the recession by having a work-in," Steve told me as we waited for the updated Hy-Sonic figures to download. "They've brought in camp beds and done a deal with the local takeaways and laundries and stuff. Those guys are working virtually every waking hour."

"That's right," Gary added, sauntering across to join our conversation, "I heard much the same thing. How we're supposed to compete with guys like that I just don't know."

"Maybe we'll have to battle them on their own terms," I suggested.

"Shh!" they both chorused.

"Don't give the bastards any more ideas," Gary continued. "It was bad enough enduring that frigging loyalty chair."

"I quite enjoyed it," I confessed.

"You would," Gary countered, "you've got a small enough brain already! Repeated exposure will soon change your mind. And everything else about you!"

They wandered off, chuckling to themselves. I tried never to let office banter get to me. I knew my commissions were well up with theirs. Salt Mine Securities had me worried, though.

Later, I asked Steve, "You know what we were talking about earlier? Well, I thought they always employed right-on family men. So how are they squaring that with the workforce?"

"They've got that covered as well, Dave. Each employee is allowed half an hour conjugal rights in the recreation room. Two point five times per week."

"Two point five? You're making this up!"

"Straight up, I'm not. Two point five is the national average. Maybe they do alternate weeks. Shit, I don't know, I'm only giving you the grapevine!"

"Apocryphal wind-ups, more like," I muttered.

I left my PC humming and wheezing to itself awhile in order to stare across the street at our unstinting rivals. With their partially grilled windows and modern employment practices, Salt Mine's plush offices resembled an air-conditioned prison.

Christine was taking a turn on reception. As much as I had a virtual mountain of vital work downloading into my machine and rendering itself semi-comprehensible on my monitor, at least a part of my cave man brain was spending all available waking hours concocting excuses to walk out to her station and engage her in flirtatious conversation. What lame justification might I unearth today to indicate my unrequited obsession with her bobbed blonde hair and so petite figure?

We were an equal opportunities employer in theory, of course, but it remains true that men and women behave differently within the workplace. Every so often the apparent working peace of our open plan abode would be fractured by unauthorised visitors from the world outside: Avon ladies, flower sellers, even once a snarling gypsy crone giving the evil eye to everybody who wouldn't shell out for her lucky heather. It was always the women who bent the company rules and let these strangers on the make cross our threshold.

This time it was a down and out peddling single dwarf roses and rather unhealthy looking bonsai trees. He stood awhile quite close to my desk gazing at the pound, dollar and Euro signs like a tribesman watching the camp fire.

"They're selling a lot of apples on Wall Street," he muttered to no one in particular. I say "down and out" but his threads looked like frayed but still serviceable Saville Row and he had the distinct air about him of having seen better days within quite recent memory. I was still unnerved and annoyed by his presence, however, whatever residual sympathy he invoked.

After he'd left, I strolled out to Christine's desk intending not to reprimand her but offer some needful advice about correct office etiquette, especially given the current jobs market. She was involved in a slightly hushed but still giggly phone conversation and refused to catch my eye.

I waited a minute or two then returned to my figures.

Even the sycophantic newspapers were starting to print something like the truth as the current government's honeymoon period fizzled out. "Second Consecutive Rise in Jobless Totals" was a sober example. "As Sleazy As The Last Lot!" was more typical. And on the inside pages, lest we had forgotten – and, of course, we *had* – a more detailed analysis of the official statistics and a reminder that there were millions ineligible for benefit and subsequent counting but still loose on the jobs market. Wages had held steady for the past two years and in several cases workers had experienced pay cuts. The occasional threat of industrial action was either laughingly dismissed by whip-handed employers or met with summary dismissal. Thus, I could hardly be blamed for keeping my head down and being grateful for what I had.

I knew that the long-term effects of the loyalty chair might be irreversibly damaging but, hey, this was financial services where you live for now and make your money while you can. Even though I would soon have to shell out for a new wardrobe, I was eminently eligible for a personal loan and that was probably the least of my worries.

I was also aware, of course, that Christine was concurrently undergoing the loyalty conditioning. This fact would doubtless bring us closer together in the fullness of time even if the ongoing treatment began to distance me from the average slaving Joe Public.

There was a run of billboard and television adverts from some bank or other urging us to "Live for the weekend". Chance would be a fine thing! Lately I'd put so much effort into the daily grind that I needed the whole of Saturday to recover. On Sunday I'd arranged to meet an old college friend for a pub lunch. The conversation faltered along for a pint or two.

"You look different," he suggested. "Not quite so... *big*, I s'pose. I used to find you quite physically imposing during the old days."

"I've got a fitness machine in my lounge," I answered, "but I don't seem to have the time or energy to use it at the moment. Bit of a self-fulfilling prophecy, I know..."

I smiled. We drained our lagers, managed a few snippets about the relative merits of various makes of mobile phones, then went our separate ways.

My renewed efforts at work have been noticed again. At just after eleven, Mr St John called me away from the over-large keys of my PC and into his plush velvet office.

"Let's have a look at that monitor," he stated, removing the blue chip from my left wrist with a pair of specially adapted pliers. He held it up to the Tiffany lamp and murmured, "Mmm, very good, David," or some such pleasantry. "Everyone will be impressed with this. Time for the chair again, methinks," he added brightly.

There was the usual sudden electric shock as I lay down in the loyalty chair but soon my eyes were closing and the only assault was from the beautiful and charming visions assailing my senses. I felt nothing of the physical constriction.

I was back at primary school with my best friend Derek. We were out on the green fields playing kiss-chase with the secret love of my seven year old self – Rachel Perry, six and a half, ginger-haired, freckly, snot-nosed and smarter than most of our incredibly elderly teachers. Derek, I noticed, was making something of a play for the more conventionally attractive Diane Farris, a tall girl from the next class up, skin smooth and brown like her father's but already possessing the lush angel fair locks of her white mother. The sun burned like Icarus in a clear blue sky and we ran, tumbled and skittered like only children can. Derek and I rested a while by the water fountain, both of us red and out of breath but bursting with innocent laughter, too. In his slightly dishevelled blazer and yellow and black tie he looked like an overworked bee.

We scooted from flower to blazing flower, our wings making a reassuringly slow drone. The nectar was sweeter than kisses. I wanted only to spend the rest of my life in that glorious garden but I knew that at some point I would be called back to the hive. A flock of birds passed overhead but their temporary shadow did not disturb me as my consciousness of time and ability to suck the sugar from each luscious moment was so much more developed...

The petals were smooth and curiously black. Unwittingly, I began to slide inwards... downwards...

When I awoke, Mr St John allowed me to rest on the seat for a few minutes before the unstrapping. When I stood up I was fully six inches shorter.

Blame my parents, but I've never learned to think in

centimetres.

I read somewhere that the average Roman soldier was not much above four and a half feet tall. Certainly our six foot six footballers, basketball stars and lads lounging about town would seem veritable giants to our ancestors. And yet as people get bigger through changes in diet, habitation and fitness the nature of our work is miniaturising. The thoughts of millions can be easily stored on a microchip no bigger than a postage stamp. Future technology will be ever smaller. The important decisions that affect the livelihoods of whole communities are merely invisible electronic impulses making a microscopic cyber-journey across a circuit board. I sit all day with one eye upon our flickering pound, dollar and Euro signs. Each change in height or intensity represents a fortune made or lost in some financial market, maybe even a whole economy going down the pan. I myself am rendered very minute by the scale of such business. All I can do is comply with whatever the company demands to keep me in solvent employment.

My great-grandfather worked on the docks. Every Monday he'd line up with thousands of others waiting for his name to be called. If he was one of that week's chosen few his family might have meat on the table by Friday; if others took his place he might go scrumping for apples or blackberries or else try to stave off his hunger with a warm pint of bitter on credit at The Duck and Diamond. What goes around comes around, I suppose, as the latest news is that all employees of Hy-Sonic are required to bid and be interviewed for their jobs at the commencement of every week.

Our loyalty chair is sorting out the men from the boys. I welcome its leather embrace. Alcohol and dope have never brought me such soft, innocent dreams. I feel young and strong again. My mind rides on candy floss clouds for that gorgeous quarter hour and, best of all, this innocent recreation is actually helping preserve my precious job and my employer's profit margins as all around us the world economy spirals into recession and the number of necessary personnel contracts.

The company needs a *smaller* workforce in order to cut costs and maximise returns to shareholders. I'm sure the situation is only temporary and one day soon we'll re-enter a period of expansion.

Until then I give up my excess baggage gladly so that I can stay, if not ahead of, at least still part of the game.

Like all gifts of the genie or genius, my size reduction has brought both benefits and difficulties. I was jeered at and briefly chased by a bunch of puffa-jacketed youths on my way back from the tube station. "Fucking rich bastard midget!" was about the most comprehensible of their angry jibes. I'm finding, also, that I can no longer easily reach the cupboards in my kitchen and the gas hob is a shade tall for my liking. Even cooking half a small can of beans can prove quite hazardous. Still, on the positive side, my ordinary TV is beginning to take on the apparent dimensions of a widescreen home cinema model and the sofa has never felt comfier.

I expect my lifestyle, however, to increase in inverse proportion to the diminution of my physical stature. Soon I trust I shall move to a smaller, cheaper apartment in a better district with neighbours who have made similar sacrifices in order to retain their gainful employment.

There was a television programme last night about the death of the dinosaurs. It was the usual claptrap about a meteor off the coast of Mexico, nuclear winters and sudden, almost overnight extinction. Do me a favour, chaps! What seems a short time in the fossil record can, in fact, last for millennia in the real world, and that's just for starters!

Remember when you were a small child? The summers were longer, the school term lasted forever, your whole time sense experienced every moment as so much more extended compared to the way years race past in adulthood. Perception of time is all to do with *size*. How else does Nature square it with the poor old mayfly that three precious minutes are its allotted span? The dinosaurs – apatosaurus, diplodocus, mamenchisaurus and others maybe even larger – simply grew so immense that the days flew by in a vegetarian haze and there just wasn't the opportunity to adapt, evolve, even breed! They grew so big that their lives passed by in the apparent blink of a reptilian eye.

It seems to me that the direction of current human culture is entirely wrong. Instead of body-building up into enormous muscular giants we should be seeking to *reduce* our mass in order to return to the evolutionary state of our possum and shrew ancestors. Take it from me: small is beautiful.

We are confined now to the third floor. The Company's successful downsizing has already led to the amalgamation of our sundry departments and the letting of the other floors to erstwhile competitors. There are bunks in the old store room for when we need a rest break on our work-in and a small fridge and state of the art microwave see to our occasional nourishment needs. There is also a television set but everybody has been too busy at their adapted PCs to care much about news and soapsud fairy tales from the outside world.

I have noticed, also, a change in my personality since the commencement of treatment. Whereas once I used to while away much of the day in bleary-eyed squalid sexual fantasies involving film stars or pretty colleagues like Christine going down upon my huge erection, now I find my libido has largely atrophied. Indeed, the very thought of touching or kissing *girls* somewhat disgusts me now, just as it did when I was a six year old boy. Interestingly, I have retained much of the knowledge and vocabulary of an adult but have managed to regain that sense of wonder not experienced for well over twenty years.

I turn to John and say, "These computers are brilliant!"

And he answers, "Yeah, Dave, they're enough excellent. We're well lucky that the big bosses are letting us have a go on them."

Mr St John had hardly used the loyalty chair, if at all. No doubt he didn't need to, but the net result was that he remained of roughly average size and therefore suitably imposing in his directorial role. He called me into his office and offered me his most ingratiating smile. For a moment I thought he was going to ask me to sit upon his knee, sonny boy, but instead he gave me a couple of cushions to equalise our differences somewhat, pursed his lips, steepled his nicotine stained fingers and eventually stated flatly:

"I have some news you may not want to hear, David."

"What's that, sir?"

"Well, it's simply that we can't let you use the loyalty chair any longer. Our medical consultants have reliably informed us that one more reduction would almost certainly kill you."

Oh no! No more innocent golden dreams sponsored by my beneficent employers!

"Please," I muttered, "isn't there any...? You know I'll do whatever is best for the company, even if it means risking my life."

He smiled. "I'm touched – yes, genuinely – that you'd be willing to make the ultimate sacrifice for Hirojima Financial but there are several insurance angles that our legal people haven't quite ironed out yet."

"Can't you reverse the process a little and then let me undergo it once more?"

"'Fraid not, Dave."

I had nothing to say for a minute or so whilst I considered the enormity of this news. Finally I asked, "So what happens now?"

"Well, Hirojima Financial needs to downsize again but this time you won't be included in the restructuring."

"Does that mean I'm out on the street?"

"Well, *technically*, yes, but we're putting together a rescue package and you'll be in line for substantial compensation, of course. Trust us, David. We honestly appreciate all your efforts and we'll do our best by you, as always."

Before I can truly comprehend how my life has down-turned, I'm out on the pavement with Gary, Christine and Steve. The facade of Hirojima Financial looms over us, a Tower of Babel, a castle of no return. For a few moments there's no one else around then suddenly – piercingly, shriekingly – the hooter sounds for the universal food break and the streets are filled with wild Brobdinagians whose gigantic feet threaten to overwhelm and trample us. I run for whatever cover I can find. I see Gary go under and consider for just a moment going back to try and help him but personal survival wins out over altruism. For now, anyway.

One of the normal sized giants stops, stoops and lifts the still lovely Christine up into his cupped hands. I think I recognise him as Mr Hirojima himself. I shout but he doesn't hear. The traffic bollard feels cold and smooth against my sensitive youthful skin. Mr Hirojima crosses the busy street and I'm glad Christine has found salvation. After all I've done to preserve the market leadership of Hirojima Financial I know they'll be back soon to rescue me from this car-fume, rat race madhouse. From the trampling hordes and the unskilled cast-offs.

Won't they?

Allen Ashley is an author, an award-winning editor, a prize-winning poet and a writing tutor. He won the British Fantasy Society Award for Best Anthology in 2006 as editor of The Elastic Book Of Numbers (Elastic Press, 2005). He leads the advanced writing group Clockhouse London Writers. He is the judge for the BFS Short Story Competition 2013.

ACKNOWLEDGEMENTS

'The Small Ones Hurt the Most' Copyright © Gary McMahon 2012.

'The Silence After Winter' Copyright © Adam Craig 2012.

'Canvassing Opinion' Copyright © Stuart Hughes 2012. Originally published in *Morpheus Tales XVII*. Reprinted by permission of the author.

'Some Girls Wander by Mistake' Copyright © Amelia Mangan 2012.

'Puppyberries' Copyright © John Greenwood 2012.

'Like Clockwork' Copyright © Benedict J. Jones 2012.

'Special Girl' Copyright © E. M. Salter 2012.

'Five an Hour' Copyright © Devan Goldstein 2012. Originally published in *PANK* magazine, February 2012 issue. Reprinted by permission of the author.

'Bred in the Bone' Copyright © Jeff Gardiner 2009. Originally published in *Twisted Tongues 12* and subsequently reprinted in *Tales of the Numinous*. Reprinted by permission of the author.

'The Algorithm' Copyright © Cameron Suey 2012.

'Against the Back Wall' Copyright © Dan Howarth 2012.

'Killer Con' Copyright © A. D. Barker 2012.

'Piranha' Copyright © Steve Byrne 2012.

'The Ballad of Bailey Blonde' Copyright © Marc Sorondo 2012.

ND - #0501 - 270225 - C0 - 229/152/15 - PB - 9781907133824 - Matt Lamination